THE
EARTH
IN THREE DIMENSIONS
WORLD ATLAS

BY KEITH LYE
MAPS BY
MALCOLM PORTER

DIAL BOOKS FOR YOUNG READERS

CONTENTS

Published by
Dial Books for Young Readers
A Division of Penguin Books USA Inc.
375 Hudson Street, New York, New York 10014

Conceived and designed by Electric Paper, London
Copyright © 1994 Electric Paper

Cartographer and
Diagram Illustrator: Malcolm Porter
Paper Engineer: David Hawcock
Picture Research: Moira McIlroy
Illustrator (endpapers): David Hardy

Printed in Colombia by Carvajal S.A.
First Edition ISBN 0-8037-1739-3

Picture acknowledgments

Airbus Industries: 20(bl). **B&C Alexander:** 11.
J.Allan Cash: 20(bc), 34(r). **Duncan Brown:** 10/11.
Colorific: 24(r). **Eurotunnel Press Office:** 20(t). **Eye
Ubiquitous:** 24(l). **Greenpeace:** 37(c). **Image Bank:**
32(r) P.Thomann. **Magnum:** 23, 37(b). **Oxford
Scientific Films:** 15(br). **Science Photo Library:**
6 5(t), 15(t), 37(t). **Spectrum Colour Library:** 8(b),
13,16(b),19(b), 25(l), 26(l), 29(t), 29(br). **Frank
Spooner Pictures:** 20(br), 15(bl) . **Tony Stone
Associates:** 6, 6/7, 7, 8(t), 9,10, 12(b), 12(t, 14(l),
14(r), 16(t), 16(c), 18(t), 18(c), 18(bl), 18(br),19(t),
21(t), 21(b), 22(t), 25(r), 26(r), 27(tl), 27(tr), 27(c),
27(b), 29(bl), 31(bl), 31(br), 32(l), 33(tl), 33(tr), 34(l),
36. **Zefa:** 5(b), 17, 22(b).

INTRODUCTION

THE EARTH IN THREE DIMENSIONS contains a pop-up globe that shows the Earth as it would look to an astronaut in a distant spacecraft. The globe shows the seven continents, listed in order of size on the facing page, and the oceans, which cover more than seven-tenths of the Earth's surface.

Like the Earth, the pop-up globe turns on its axis, an imaginary line running from the North Pole through the center of the Earth to the South Pole. The globe also shows the location of the Equator, an imaginary circle around the Earth, exactly halfway between the two poles.

The Atlas
THE EARTH IN THREE DIMENSIONS also includes a World Atlas that contains detailed maps of the continents, plus information about countries, capitals and other large cities, rivers, lakes, and mountains. All of the world's independent countries are shown on the Atlas's maps. You will discover how the boundaries of some countries have changed, because of wars and differences in political or religious beliefs.

How to Use This Atlas
To find out what the symbols and colors on the maps mean, see the key on page 3. Pages containing the map of a continent also have a small "locater globe" with the continent shown in yellow. This will help you locate the continent on the pop-up globe. Use the scale bars to work out distances between places on the maps. A table listing the area, population, and capital of every country in the world begins on page 38.

Key to the maps

	Forests
	Farmland/Pastures
	Deserts
	Tundra
	Icepack

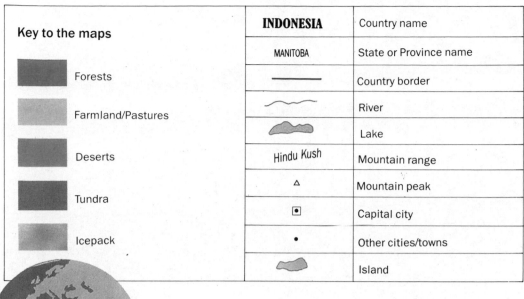

INDONESIA	Country name
MANITOBA	State or Province name
———	Country border
	River
	Lake
Hindu Kush	Mountain range
△	Mountain peak
⊡	Capital city
•	Other cities/towns
	Island

miles
0 — 500
0 — 500
kilometers

△ *You will find these colors and symbols on each map, and this chart tells you what they mean.*

△ *Scale bar*
◁ *Locater globe*

△ *This map projection shows all the continents in the world, but its flat picture is not accurate.*
▽ *A globe gives an accurate picture of Earth, but because it is shaped like the planet shows only part of the Earth at any one time.*

Maps and Globes

Globes give a true and accurate picture of our Earth. But globes are small. They cannot give us as much information as maps. Maps can also be used to give special information, such as the extent of pollution around the world, as shown on the world maps on pages 36–37. But mapmakers face a problem. There is no way of showing the curved surface of the Earth on a flat piece of paper without distorting it in some way. For example, the oval world map, at left, could not fully cover the surface of a globe.

Map Projections

Mapmakers have worked out ways of showing the world, or parts of it, as accurately as possible on flat surfaces. These are called map projections. By using map projections, which are worked out mathematically, mapmakers can show some features, such as areas, shapes, and distances, accurately. But some parts of the world have to be distorted in order to show a world map in one piece.

The Continents in brief

Asia: *area* 17,006,000 sq mi (44,045,000 sq km) *population* 3,307,000,000

Africa: *area* 11,684,000 sq mi (30,261,000 sq km) *population* 664,000,000

North America: *area* 9,358,000 sq mi (24,237,000 sq km) *population* 433,000,000

South America: *area* 6,875,000 sq mi (17,806,000 sq km) *population* 304,000,000

Antarctica: *area* 5,400,000 sq mi (14,000,000 sq km) *population* none permanent

Europe: *area* 4,062,000 sq mi (10,521,000 sq km) *population* 700,000,000

Australia: *area* 2,978,000 sq mi (7,713,000 sq km) *population* 17,500,000

Latitude and Longitude

Every place on Earth can be located by imaginary lines called latitudes and longitudes. Latitude lines run east to west across maps and globes. They are measured in degrees north or south of 0° latitude, or the Equator, which lies exactly halfway between the North and South poles. Longitude lines run north to south, passing through the poles. They are measured in degrees east or west of 0° longitude, or the Prime Meridian, which passes through London, England.

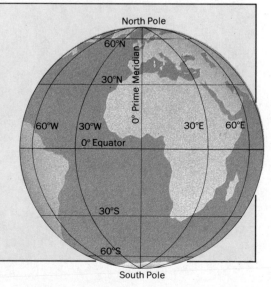

OUR CHANGING WORLD

SCIENTISTS BELIEVE that 500 million years ago the Earth's land areas were very different from those of today. At that time there may have been only four continents. Over millions of years the ancient landmasses moved slowly toward one another. Around 250 million years ago they came together to form a single continent called Pangaea (pan-GEE-uh).

Laurasia and Gondwanaland

About 180 million years ago Pangaea began to break apart. A large piece of it split away and drifted north. Scientists call this Laurasia. What remained of Pangaea is called Gondwanaland.

Over the last 135 million years Laurasia and Gondwanaland have broken apart too, and formed the seven continents of the modern world. North America, Europe, and most of Asia were once part of Laurasia. Gondwanaland split into what is now South America, Africa, India, Australia, and Antarctica.

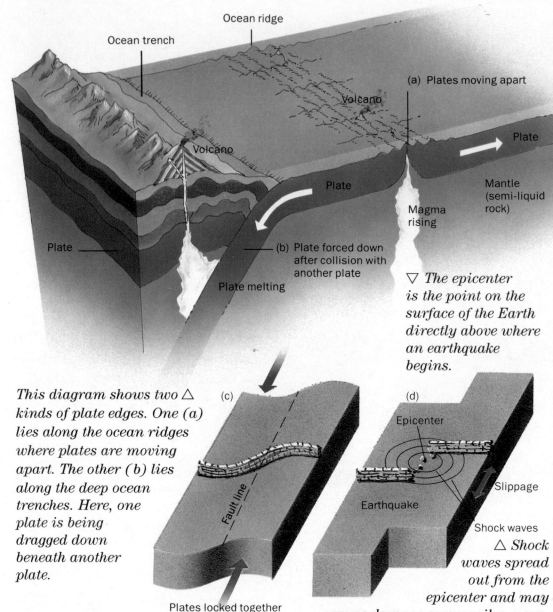

This diagram shows two △ kinds of plate edges. One (a) lies along the ocean ridges where plates are moving apart. The other (b) lies along the deep ocean trenches. Here, one plate is being dragged down beneath another plate.

▽ *The epicenter is the point on the surface of the Earth directly above where an earthquake begins.*

△ *Shock waves spread out from the epicenter and may cause damage many miles away.*

△ *Some plates move alongside each other in opposite directions (c). This is called a transform fault. Earthquakes occur when the plates move with a sudden jerk (d).*

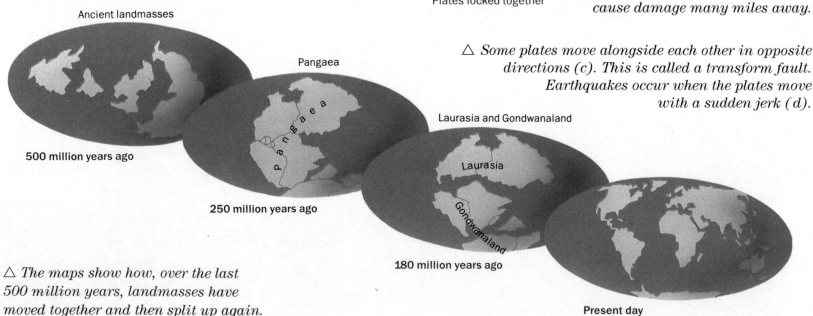

Ancient landmasses

500 million years ago

Pangaea

250 million years ago

Laurasia and Gondwanaland

Laurasia

Gondwanaland

180 million years ago

Present day

△ *The maps show how, over the last 500 million years, landmasses have moved together and then split up again.*

4

Moving Plates

Landmasses can shift because the Earth's hard outer crust is split like a cracked eggshell into large blocks or plates. The plates form the continents and ocean floors.

Under the plates, between 43 and 62 miles (70–100 kilometers) below the surface, is a thick layer of semi-liquid rock called the mantle. Great heat from the Earth's core creates currents in the mantle, which cause the plates to shift position. These shifts result in earthquakes, volcanic eruptions, and the formation of

it begins to melt. The collision forms a deep trench in the ocean floor.

At the same time melted rock is pushed up against the crust and may form a volcanic mountain on dry land. When pressure from the molten rock becomes too great, the volcano erupts, spewing magma, called lava on land, from its top.

Earthquakes

The Earth's plates do not move smoothly. Most of the time their jagged edges are locked together,

pressing hard against each other. When the pressure becomes too great, the plates shift suddenly and cause earthquakes.

Earthquakes are common around ocean ridges and trenches. They also occur along cracks in the Earth's surface called transform faults. These cracks form where two plates are moving past each other in opposite directions. The San Andreas Fault in California is a transform fault. Movements along this fault cause earthquakes from Los Angeles to San Francisco.

Mountains

Mountains are formed when plates collide. "Fold mountains" occur when two plates push against each other, squeezing the rocks between them into huge folds. The world's highest range, the Himalayas, was formed when a plate carrying India pushed against the Eurasian plate. Plate movements also fracture — crack — rocks. Blocks of rock pushed up along the faults form "block mountains."

▽ A volcano in Russia's Kamchatka peninsula is one of many that circle the Pacific Ocean. These volcanoes form the huge Pacific "ring of fire."

mountain ranges.

Ocean Ridges

The flowing mantle can slowly pull plates apart. When this happens on the ocean floor, semi-liquid rock called magma rises up between the plates. The magma cools and hardens to form underwater mountain ridges.

Ocean Trenches

When two plates collide underwater, the edge of one is pushed beneath the other and forced into the hot mantle where

△ Movement along the plate edges of the San Andreas Fault has caused major earthquakes, most recently in Los Angeles in 1994. In 1906 the plate edges moved up to 18 feet (5.5 meters) in opposite directions, causing an earthquake that destroyed San Francisco.

THE NORTH POLE AND THE ARCTIC

THE ARCTIC includes the Arctic Ocean, the world's smallest ocean, and those parts of Asia, Europe, and North America that lie within the Arctic Circle. The North Pole lies near the center of the Arctic Ocean. The Arctic has long, bitterly cold winters. Sea ice, which is often called pack ice, covers much of the ocean throughout the year. Greenland, the world's largest

miles
0   500

0   500
kilometers

△ *Polar bears live in the icy Arctic region, hunting seals and other animals for food.*

The Arctic Ocean in brief

Area: about 3,668,000 sq mi (about 9,500,000 sq km)
Greatest known depth: about 18,045 feet (about 5,500 meters)
Permanent ice cover: about 2,316,600 sq mi (about 6,000,000 sq km)
Thickness of sea ice: 10–12 feet (3–3.5 meters)

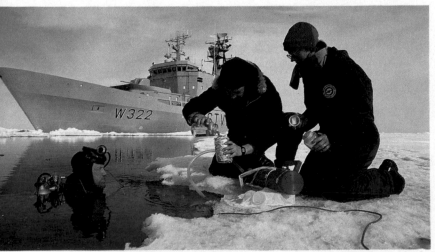

◁ *Scientists work in the cold waters of the Arctic Ocean, recording weather conditions, water temperatures, movements of ice, and evidence of pollution.*

island, lies in the Arctic. Most of Greenland, like many other Arctic islands, is covered by ice and snow throughout the year. The Arctic also includes a treeless region called the tundra, where the snow does melt in summer. Plants such as lichens, mosses, low shrubs, and nearly 1,000 kinds of flowers grow in the tundra region. Animals such as caribou, reindeer, and moose graze there during the summer. The Inuit people, also known as Eskimos, live in the Arctic regions of North America.

THE SOUTH POLE AND ANTARCTICA

ANTARCTICA, the world's fifth largest continent, is bigger than either Europe or Australia. Antarctica surrounds the South Pole and is the coldest continent. The lowest known air temperature, -128.6°F (-89.2°C), was recorded there in 1983.

Most of Antarctica is covered by ice, which is up to 15,750 feet (4,800 meters) thick in places. In some areas the ice extends over the sea, forming ice shelves. Chunks of the ice that break away are called icebergs. One such iceberg was as big as the states of Maryland and Delaware combined.

The Antarctic Peninsula, which points toward South America, has some ice-free areas where the

△ *Sea ice surrounds much of Antarctica for most of the year.*

continent's only flowering plants are found. No one lives in Antarctica all the time, but scientists from several nations spend periods there in research stations. They study Antarctica's resources and the wealth of living creatures such as fish, seals, and whales found in the waters around the continent. They also record changes in weather that may affect other parts of the world.

No one owns the land in Antarctica, though several nations claim some areas. The continent has not been developed, though it contains rich mineral resources. Many people would like it to remain a wilderness, or a "world park," where its animals, including many kinds of penguins, can live in safety.

Antarctic Circle

Weddell Sea

Coats Land

Dronning Maud Land

Enderby Land

Antarctic Peninsula

Ellsworth Land

Ronne Ice Shelf

Vinson Massif
Ellsworth Mts

ANTARCTICA

South Pole

Transantarctic Mts

Wilhelm II Coast

Marie Byrd Land

Ross Ice Shelf

Mt Erebus

Wilkes Land

Victoria Land

Ross Sea

miles
0   500

0   500
kilometers

Antarctica in brief

Highest point: Vinson Massif, 16,864 feet (5,140 meters) above sea level
Greatest depth of ice: about 15,750 feet (4,800 meters)

NORTH AMERICA

NORTH AMERICA is the third largest continent after Asia and Africa. It covers about a sixth of the world's land area.

The northern part of North America includes two vast countries, Canada and the United States. In the far northeast lies Greenland, a former Danish colony that is now self-governing.

North America also includes Mexico, the seven countries of Central America that form a land bridge between Mexico and Colombia in South America, and the many tropical islands in the Caribbean Sea. North America is bounded by three oceans, the icy Arctic Ocean in the north, the Pacific Ocean in the west, and the Atlantic Ocean in the east.

North America
(2 countries)
Canada
United States of America (U.S.A.)

◁ Inuit people live in northern Canada. They catch fish through holes in the ice that covers the sea.

North America in brief

Highest point: Mount McKinley, Alaska, 20,320 feet (6,194 meters)
Longest river: Mississippi, 2,340 mi (3,766 km)
Largest lake: Lake Superior, 31,700 sq mi (82,103 sq km)

Protecting the Wilderness

Arches National Park in southeastern Utah contains beautiful natural rock formations, such as the Delicate Arch, left. Much of the finest scenery in the United States is now protected in the country's 50 national parks or in smaller areas, such as national monuments. Yellowstone National Park, established in 1870, was the world's first national park.

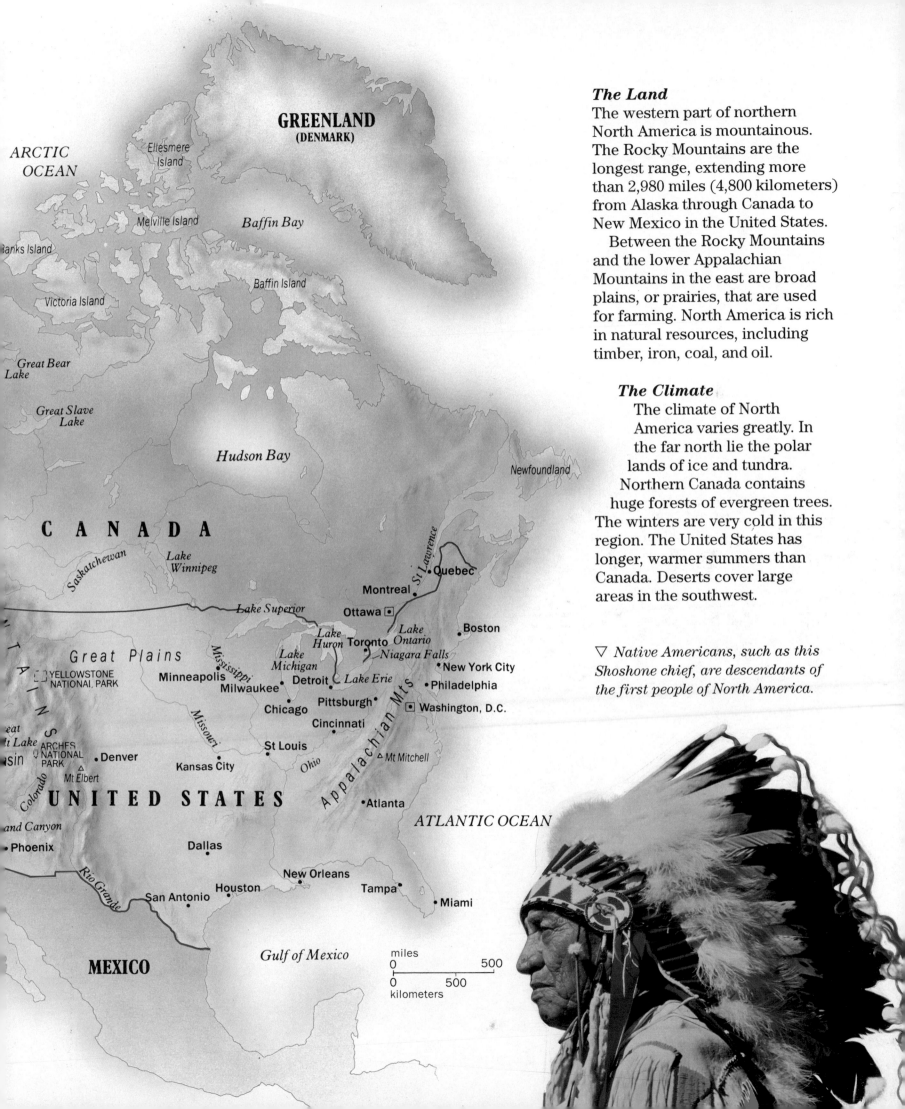

GREENLAND
(DENMARK)

*ARCTIC
OCEAN*

*Ellesmere
Island*

Melville Island

Baffin Bay

Banks Island

Victoria Island

Baffin Island

*Great Bear
Lake*

*Great Slave
Lake*

Hudson Bay

Newfoundland

C A N A D A

Saskatchewan *Lake
Winnipeg*

Lake Superior

St Lawrence

● Quebec

Montreal ●

Ottawa ⊡

*Lake
Huron* Toronto *Lake
Ontario*

● Boston

Great Plains

*Lake
Michigan* Niagara Falls

■ YELLOWSTONE
NATIONAL PARK

Mississippi

Minneapolis

Milwaukee

Detroit *Lake Erie*

Pittsburgh

● New York City

● Philadelphia

Chicago

⊡ Washington, D.C.

Cincinnati

Missouri

St Louis

Ohio

eat
t Lake

ARCHES
NATIONAL
PARK

● Denver

Kansas City

△ Mt Mitchell

sin

Mt Elbert

U N I T E D   S T A T E S

Appalachian Mts

Colorado

● Atlanta

ATLANTIC OCEAN

nd Canyon

● Phoenix

Dallas

New Orleans

Houston

Tampa ●

San Antonio

Rio Grande

● Miami

MEXICO

Gulf of Mexico

miles
0 ——————— 500
0 ——————— 500
kilometers

The Land
The western part of northern
North America is mountainous.
The Rocky Mountains are the
longest range, extending more
than 2,980 miles (4,800 kilometers)
from Alaska through Canada to
New Mexico in the United States.
   Between the Rocky Mountains
and the lower Appalachian
Mountains in the east are broad
plains, or prairies, that are used
for farming. North America is rich
in natural resources, including
timber, iron, coal, and oil.

The Climate
   The climate of North
America varies greatly. In
the far north lie the polar
lands of ice and tundra.
Northern Canada contains
huge forests of evergreen trees.
The winters are very cold in this
region. The United States has
longer, warmer summers than
Canada. Deserts cover large
areas in the southwest.

▽ *Native Americans, such as this
Shoshone chief, are descendants of
the first people of North America.*

CANADA

CANADA is the world's second largest country after the Russian Federation (Russia). It stretches right across North America, between the North Pacific and North Atlantic Oceans.

Canada is a vast country, but about 80 percent of the people live within 186 miles (300 kilometers) of the U.S. border. Far northern Canada is too cold for human settlement.

Canada is divided into ten provinces and two territories, each with its own government. The national Parliament meets in Ottawa, the country's capital. Canada was once part of the British Empire. The people still have strong ties with the United Kingdom and they recognize Queen Elizabeth II as their head of state. The country became self-governing in 1867.

Canada also has strong ties with the United States. In 1994 Canada, the United States, and Mexico signed the North American Free Trade Agreement, which has created a huge trading union.

The People
The first people to settle in North America were the ancestors of the Native Americans (also called American Indians). They entered North America from Asia about 40,000 years ago, when

Canadian provinces and capitals

YUKON TERRITORY
Whitehorse

NORTHWEST TERRITORIES
Yellowknife

BRITISH COLUMBIA

ALBERTA
Edmonton

Victoria

SASKATCHEWAN
Regina

MANITOBA
Winnipeg

ONTARIO

NEWFOUNDLAND
St John's

QUEBEC

Quebec

PRINCE EDWARD ISLAND
Charlottetown

Fredericton
NEW BRUNSWICK

NOVA SCOTIA
Halifax

Great Lakes
Ottawa

Toronto

the sea level was lower than it is today and the continents were joined by a land bridge.

The Native Americans spread southward throughout North and South America. Later arrivals, the ancestors of the Inuit people, also came from Asia, but they stayed in the north in what is now Canada

◁ *Quebec is Canada's oldest city and the capital of French-speaking Quebec province.*

and Alaska. Today, the Native Americans, including the Inuit, make up only about two percent of Canada's population. The majority of the people are of European descent. About 37 percent of Canadians are of British descent. They speak English, one of Canada's two official languages.

The other official language is French, since about 32 percent of Canadians are of French descent. Quebec has the largest French-speaking population, and many of its residents have said that they want to establish their own independent country.

Other large groups of people are of German, Italian, and Ukrainian descent. In recent years many Asian emigrants have settled in Canada.

◁ *Grouse Mountain is a ski resort on Vancouver's north shore. Vancouver, one of Canada's largest cities, is a major port in the province of British Columbia.*

The Economy
Canada has plenty of fertile farmland, vast forests, and rich reserves of many minerals. It is a wealthy country and its people enjoy high standards of living. About 77 percent of Canadians live in cities and towns. The largest cities, Toronto and Montreal, are in the country's main industrial region that lies near the Great Lakes and in the St. Lawrence River valley.

ALASKA

ALASKA is the largest state in the United States. But it ranks 49th in population. Only Wyoming has fewer people.

Nearly a third of Alaska lies in the Arctic region. Winters are long and cold, but some crops can grow during the short summers. Large areas of wilderness have been set aside as national parks. The Denali National Park includes Mount McKinley, the highest mountain in North America.

Southern Alaska and the Aleutian Islands contain active volcanoes. The area is also hit from time to time by severe earthquakes.

The People
Approximately 550,000 people live in Alaska. This figure includes about 74,000 Native Americans — 50,000 Inuit and 24,000 American Indians. Most of the other people who live in Alaska are of European descent.

The 49th State
The western tip of mainland Alaska is only 51 miles (82 kilometers) from Russia, which once owned Alaska. But in 1867 the United States bought the territory for $7.2 million.

Many Americans thought that this was a waste of money. The purchase of Alaska was called Seward's Folly, after William H. Seward, the American Secretary of State who was responsible for buying the area. But Alaska's rich resources, including oil, minerals, and timber, have repaid the purchase price many times over.

Alaska finally became a state of the United States on January 3, 1959. It became the 49th state seven months before Hawaii achieved statehood as the 50th state on August 21, 1959.

▽ *Sleds drawn by husky dogs are sometimes still used for transport in Alaska and northern Canada.*

THE UNITED STATES AND HAWAII

THE UNITED STATES of America is the world's fourth largest country, after Russia, Canada, and China. It is divided into 50 states, each of which has its own government. The national government is based in the country's capital, Washington, D.C. The letters D.C. stand for the District of Columbia, a special area that was set aside for the capital city.

During the 16th and 17th centuries many Europeans migrated to North America and settled. The British gradually gained control over much of North America. The United States was created when American colonists fought the War of Independence against British control. The war officially ended in 1783.

The new nation grew rapidly during the 19th century. Today it ranks third after China and India in population. The United States is world renowned for its many achievements in the fields of science, technology, and entertainment; for example, the space program based at Cape Canaveral in Florida and the Hollywood film industry.

Hawaii

Hawaii became the 50th state of America in 1959. It is the only state that is not on the North American mainland.

Hawaii consists of 8 large and 124 small islands that lie in the North Pacific Ocean. All the islands are formed by volcanoes that rise from the sea floor.

The only active volcanoes today are on the largest island, which is also called Hawaii. Hawaii is a beautiful state that attracts many tourists. The original people of Hawaii were Polynesians, but today people of Polynesian descent make up only about 15 percent of the population. People descended from Europeans and Japanese and other Asians make up the rest. The capital of the state is Honolulu, on Oahu Island.

▽ Buffalo once roamed on the prairies where wheat is now grown on highly efficient farms.

△ California's redwoods are the tallest trees in the world. The tallest tree on earth is a redwood named "Howard A. Libby."

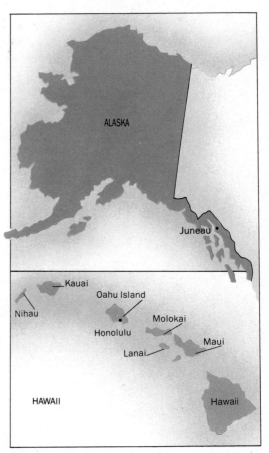

The People

Native Americans, the first people in North America, now make up less than 1 percent of the population of the United States, while people of European origin, who began to settle in the 16th century, make up about 80 percent.

African Americans are the largest minority group in the United States, making up about 12 percent of the population. Other groups include people who have come—or whose ancestors have come—from Asia, Mexico, and various Pacific and Caribbean islands.

The Economy

The United States is a rich country. It produces more agricultural products, including corn, wheat, and soybeans, than any other country in the world.

Most people live in cities, where they work in manufacturing and service industries. Pittsburgh, Pennsylvania, with its many iron, steel, and chemical plants, is one of the largest industrial cities in the northeast. The computer industry is concentrated in California. Detroit, Michigan, is known as the automobile capital of the world, producing 25 percent of the world's cars and trucks.

The country's largest cities include New York City, Los Angeles, Chicago, Houston, and Philadelphia.

▷ *The New York City skyline by night is one of the world's most glittering sights.*

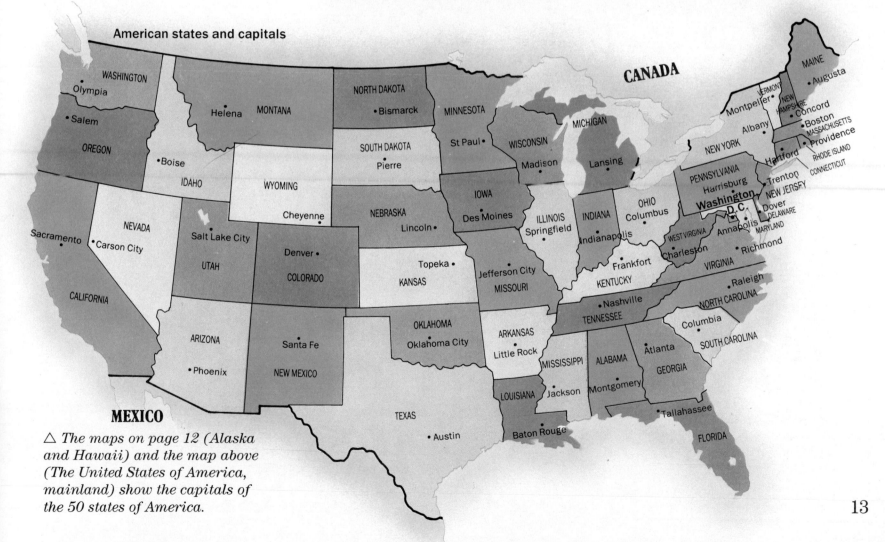

American states and capitals

△ *The maps on page 12 (Alaska and Hawaii) and the map above (The United States of America, mainland) show the capitals of the 50 states of America.*

13

MEXICO, CENTRAL AND SOUTH AMERICA, AND THE CARIBBEAN

THE HUGE REGION extending from Mexico to the tip of South America, is called Latin America. This is because most people speak Spanish, French, or Portuguese languages that developed from Latin, the language of ancient Rome. A few non-Latin European languages and many Native American languages are spoken in some areas.

Mexico and Central America

The land in Mexico and Central America is mainly mountainous, with high volcanoes.

Northern Mexico contains deserts, but the climate of most of the region is warm and rainy. Mexico City is one of the largest cities in the world.

The Caribbean

The islands of the Caribbean, which are also called the West Indies, have a warm climate. Farming is a major activity, but tourism is also important. Tourists are attracted by the beaches, the magnificent scenery, and the fine weather.

Mexico, Central and South America, and the Caribbean
(33 countries)

Antigua & Barbuda	Haiti
Argentina	Honduras
Bahamas	Jamaica
Barbados	Mexico
Belize	Nicaragua
Bolivia	Panama
Brazil	Paraguay
Chile	Peru
Colombia	St. Kitts-
Costa Rica	Nevis
Cuba	St. Lucia
Dominica	St. Vincent
Dominican	& the
Republic	Grenadines
Ecuador	Suriname
El Salvador	Trinidad
Grenada	& Tobago
Guatemala	Uruguay
Guyana	Venezuela

South America

South America, the fourth largest continent, contains the world's longest mountain chain, the Andes.

The climate varies greatly — hot rain forests in the north, deserts on the coasts of northern Chile and Peru, and grasslands in the south. The far south contains a cold desert region called Patagonia. Sugarcane, tobacco, and coffee are grown on large plantations. South America also has natural reserves of gold, silver, copper, tin, and lead.

South America in brief

Highest point: Aconcagua, Argentina, 22,831 feet (6,959 meters)

Longest river: Amazon, 4,000 mi (6,437 km)

Largest lake: Lake Maracaibo, Venezuela, 5,217 sq mi (13,512 sq km)

△ *Before the Panama Canal was completed in 1914, ships sailing between the Atlantic and Pacific Oceans traveled around South America. The canal shortened the journey between New York City and San Francisco by 7,830 miles (12,600 kilometers).*

Native American Civilizations

Several Native American civilizations existed in Central and South America long before the arrival of Europeans. The Mayans and Toltecs built pyramids with temples on top of them in Mexico and parts of Central America. Chichén Itzá in Mexico, below, is a fine example of a Mayan city.

14

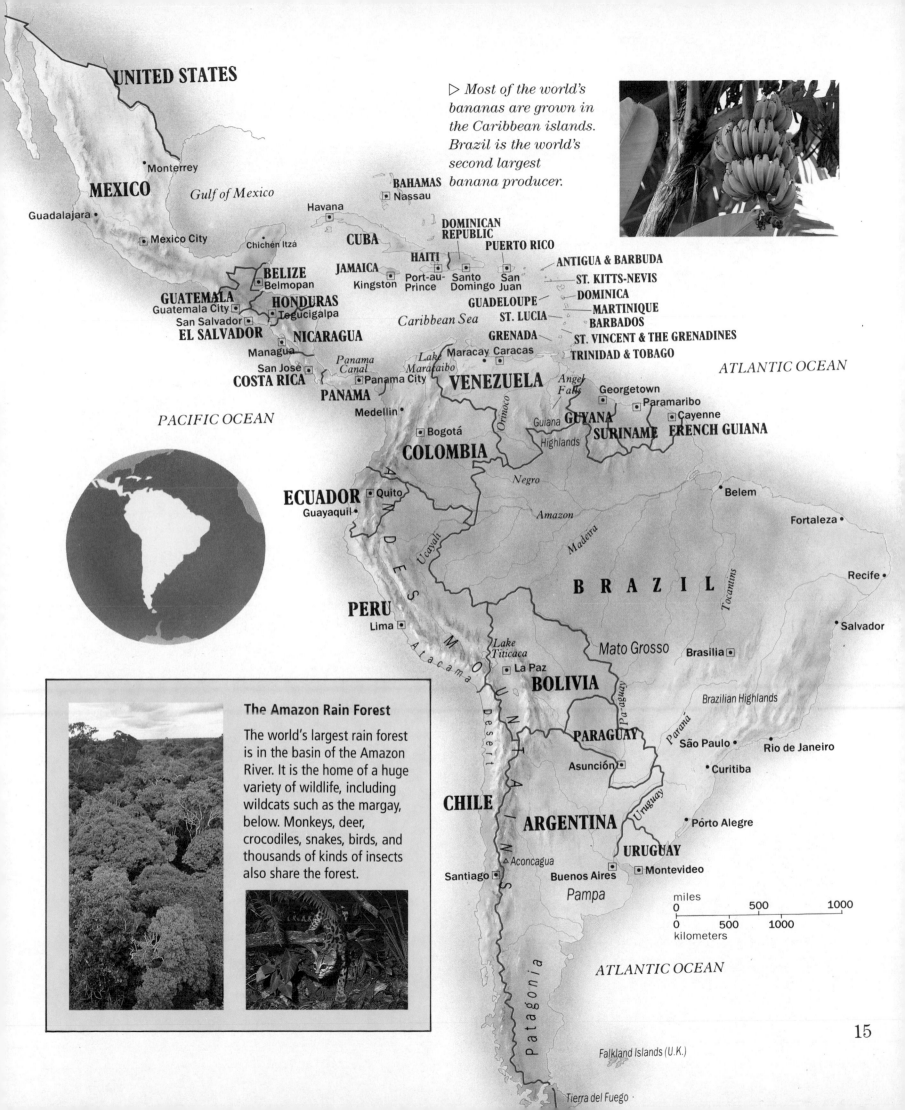

UNITED STATES

Monterrey

MEXICO

Gulf of Mexico

Guadalajara

Mexico City

Chichén Itzá

BAHAMAS
Nassau

Havana

CUBA

DOMINICAN
REPUBLIC

PUERTO RICO

HAITI

BELIZE
Belmopan

JAMAICA
Kingston

Port-au-
Prince

Santo
Domingo

San
Juan

ANTIGUA & BARBUDA

ST. KITTS-NEVIS

DOMINICA

GUATEMALA
Guatemala City

HONDURAS
Tegucigalpa

GUADELOUPE

MARTINIQUE

San Salvador

Caribbean Sea

ST. LUCIA

BARBADOS

EL SALVADOR

NICARAGUA

GRENADA

ST. VINCENT & THE GRENADINES

Managua

Maracay Caracas

TRINIDAD & TOBAGO

San José

*Panama
Canal*

Lake
Maracaibo

COSTA RICA

PANAMA

Panama City

VENEZUELA

*Angel
Falls*

Georgetown

ATLANTIC OCEAN

Medellín

Orinoco

Paramaribo

Guiana

GUYANA

Cayenne

PACIFIC OCEAN

Bogotá

Highlands

SURINAME

FRENCH GUIANA

COLOMBIA

Negro

Belem

ECUADOR

Quito

Amazon

Fortaleza

Guayaquil

Madeira

Ucayali

B R A Z I L

Recife

PERU

Lima

Tocantins

Salvador

Lake
Titicaca

Mato Grosso

Brasília

La Paz

BOLIVIA

Brazilian Highlands

Paraguay

PARAGUAY

Paraná

São Paulo

Rio de Janeiro

Asunción

Curitiba

CHILE

ARGENTINA

Uruguay

Pórto Alegre

URUGUAY

Montevideo

△ Aconcagua

Santiago

Buenos Aires

Pampa

Atacama Desert

A N D E S   M O U N T A I N S

Patagonia

ATLANTIC OCEAN

Falkland Islands (U.K.)

Tierra del Fuego

▷ *Most of the world's
bananas are grown in
the Caribbean islands.
Brazil is the world's
second largest
banana producer.*

The Amazon Rain Forest

The world's largest rain forest
is in the basin of the Amazon
River. It is the home of a huge
variety of wildlife, including
wildcats such as the margay,
below. Monkeys, deer,
crocodiles, snakes, birds, and
thousands of kinds of insects
also share the forest.

miles
0   500   1000
0   500   1000
kilometers

15

EUROPE

EUROPE is the sixth largest continent, but in population it ranks second among the seven continents after Asia.

Europe contains 39 complete independent nations, as well as 25 percent of Russia and 3 percent of Turkey. Russia is by far the largest country in Europe. Like Ukraine, Europe's second largest country,

◁ *Buckingham Palace, home of the British Royal Family, is in London, the capital of the United Kingdom. The palace, completed in 1836, has 600 rooms including a ballroom 111 feet (34 meters) long.*

Europe in brief

Highest point: Mount Elbrus, in the Caucasus Mountains, Russia, 18,481 feet (5,633 meters)

Longest river: Volga, in Russia, 2,194 mi (3,531 km)

Largest lake: Caspian Sea, which lies partly in Europe and partly in Asia, 143,630 sq mi (372,000 sq km)

part of the Soviet Union. (They, along with Russia and Ukraine, are shown in greater detail on the map on pages 22–23.)

European Mini States
Europe contains some very tiny countries. Vatican City, which covers only 0.17 square miles (0.44 square kilometers) in the Italian capital city of Rome,

(Continued on page 18)

△ *Flowers grown in the Netherlands are sold in countries all over the world.*

it was formerly part of the Soviet Union. Other large countries in Europe include France, Spain, Sweden, Norway, and Germany.

The Map of Europe
The map on page 17 shows 39 of Europe's countries, including Estonia, Latvia, and Lithuania. These 3 countries were part of the Soviet Union from 1940 to 1991. Two other European countries, Belarus and Moldova, were also

△ *Completed in 1889, the Eiffel Tower in Paris was the tallest structure in the world until 1931.*

16

Europe (39 countries)

Albania	Liechtenstein
Andorra	Lithuania
Austria	Luxembourg
Belgium	Macedonia
Bosnia &	Malta
Hercegovina	Monaco
Bulgaria	Netherlands
Croatia	Norway
Czech Republic	Poland
Denmark	Portugal
Estonia	Romania
Finland	San Marino
France	Slovakia
Germany	Slovenia
Greece	Spain
Hungary	Sweden
Iceland	Switzerland
Ireland	United Kingdom
Italy	Vatican City
Latvia	Yugoslavia*

*Yugoslavia now comprises Serbia and Montenegro only

Reykjavik
ICELAND

*◁ Europe has
many resources,
including oil
and gas deposits
under the
North Sea.*

Norwegian Sea

miles
0   500
0   500
kilometers

Faroe Is.

North Cape

NORWAY   **FINLAND**

ATLANTIC OCEAN

Oslo   **SWEDEN**   Helsinki

Stockholm   Tallinn   **RUSSIAN
                                             FEDERATION**

SCOTLAND   **ESTONIA**
Edinburgh
N. IRELAND   *North Sea*   **LATVIA**
Belfast   Riga
IRELAND   **UNITED**   **DENMARK**
                 KINGDOM   Copenhagen   *Baltic Sea*   **LITHUANIA**
Dublin
                                                   Kaliningrad   Vilnius
WALES   **(RUSSIA)**
Cardiff   **ENGLAND**   **NETHERLANDS**   Hamburg   **BELARUS**
          London   Amsterdam   Berlin
                                                        Warsaw
                        Brussels   *Elbe*
                        BELGIUM   Bonn   **GERMANY**   **POLAND**
                                      Rhine
                        LUXEMBOURG   **UKRAINE**
                         Paris   Prague
                                              CZECH REP.
                       LIECHTENSTEIN Munich   **SLOVAKIA**
Loire   Vienna   Bratislava   *Carpathian Mountains*
        FRANCE   Bern   **AUSTRIA**   Budapest   **MOLDOVA**
Bay of Biscay   **SWITZERLAND**
                 Lyon   **SLOVENIA** **HUNGARY**
                      Rhône Mt Blanc Ljubljana   Zagreb   **ROMANIA**
                                         Po   **CROATIA**   Bucharest
                              ITALY   **BOSNIA &**   Belgrade
PORTUGAL   *Pyrenees* **ANDORRA**   **HERCEGOVINA**   *Danube*
                          Marseille **MONACO**   Sarajevo
          Madrid   **SAN MARINO**   **YUGOSLAVIA**   **BULGARIA**
Tagus   Sofia
Lisbon   Barcelona   *Corsica*   Skopje
          SPAIN   Rome   Tiranë **MACEDONIA**
Ebro   **VATICAN**   **ALBANIA**   **TURKEY**
                          CITY   **GREECE**
          Gibraltar   *Balearic Is.*   *Sardinia*
          (U.K.)
                          Mediterranean Sea
                                                                       Athens
A F R I C A   *Sicily*   **MALTA**
                                                                         Crete

◁ *The Rhine, which flows through Germany, is one of Europe's most important waterways. Barges carry raw materials to factories and transport goods to the sea. Many ancient castles can be seen on the banks of the river.*

▽ *Deep valleys called fjords run far inland along Norway's coasts. These scenic valleys were worn away by rivers of ice called glaciers.*

The Land and Climate

Southern Europe has fine scenery and high mountain ranges. The highest range, the Alps, runs from France, through Switzerland, Italy, and southern Germany, into Austria.

A broad plain stretches across central Europe, from northern France through north-central Europe to the Ural Mountains in Russia. To the north, Norway and Sweden have mountains, but Finland is low-lying, with many sparkling lakes and thick forests.

The climate varies greatly from the warm lands around the Mediterranean Sea to the icy Arctic region in the north. Europe's western coasts have a mild climate, by contrast with the hot summers and bitterly cold winters in the east.

is the world's smallest independent country. It is the world headquarters of the Roman Catholic Church and it is ruled by the Pope. Monaco, Europe's second smallest country, is a tiny resort area on the southeast coast of France. The third smallest country, San Marino, is the world's oldest republic. It lies in northeastern Italy.

▽ *Although Spain is now swiftly modernizing, its old towns and cities reflect its rich and varied past.*

▽ *Venice, in northeastern Italy, is a city built on islands in the Adriatic Sea. The people use boats instead of buses to get around.*

The People

The European part of Russia contains about 120 million people. Germany, with about 80 million people, has Europe's second largest population.

About 50 languages are spoken in Europe. The main language groups are: the Romance languages, including French, Italian, Romanian, and Spanish; the Germanic languages, including

△ *Athens in Greece contains the ruins of the Parthenon, a temple built by the ancient Greeks.*

Danish, English, German, and Swedish; and the Balto-Slavic languages, including Bulgarian, Czech, Polish, and Russian.

Christianity is Europe's main religion, with Roman Catholics forming the largest group. Members of Orthodox Christian churches live mainly in the southeast and east, including Russia. Europe also has many Protestants, Muslims, Jews, and people of other faiths.

Europe has beautiful cities where old buildings stand next to modern ones. Some cities in southern Europe have ruins from great civilizations, such as ancient Greece and Rome.

The Economy

Europe's many resources include coal, oil, natural gas, and many

metals. Some countries, such as Belgium, France, Germany, Italy, the Netherlands, Spain, Sweden, and the United Kingdom, have large industries, making such things as aircraft, cars, chemicals, machinery, and textiles. Some people still make a living from farming, growing barley, fruits, potatoes, sugar beets, wheat, and other crops. Tourism is a major industry.

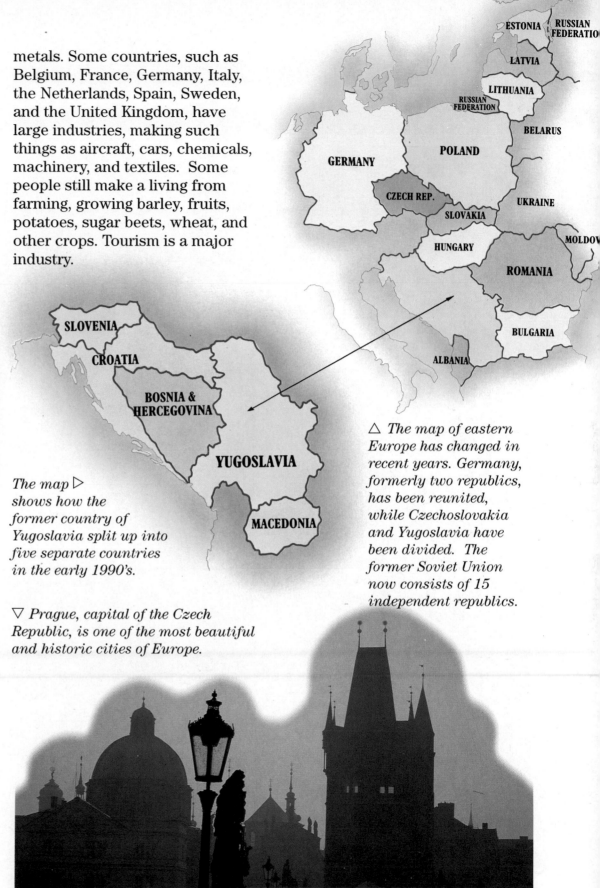

The map ▷ shows how the former country of Yugoslavia split up into five separate countries in the early 1990's.

▽ *Prague, capital of the Czech Republic, is one of the most beautiful and historic cities of Europe.*

△ *The map of eastern Europe has changed in recent years. Germany, formerly two republics, has been reunited, while Czechoslovakia and Yugoslavia have been divided. The former Soviet Union now consists of 15 independent republics.*

19

THE CHANGING FACE OF EUROPE

THE END OF World War II in 1945 brought about dramatic changes in Europe. The boundaries of several countries were changed, and millions of refugees wandered around the continent seeking new homes.

In the late 1940's the countries of Europe became divided into groups — the East and the West. Communist governments, having strong links to the former Soviet Union, took control of Albania,

Bulgaria, Czechoslovakia, East Germany, Hungary, Poland, Romania, and Yugoslavia.

The border between the Western nations and the Communist East was called the Iron Curtain because it was difficult for anyone to pass over to the West from what became known as the Eastern Bloc.

Europe Rebuilds

By the end of the war the economies of many European countries were ruined. The United States provided aid, but progress was slow as Europeans worked to rebuild their countries.

In 1952 Belgium, France, Italy, Luxembourg, the Netherlands, and West Germany set up the European Coal and Steel Community (ECSC) in an effort to restore their industries.

The European Community

In 1957 the success of the ECSC led the six countries to form the European Economic Community (EEC). The EEC worked to remove barriers that prevented movement of goods and workers between the countries. In this way they could compete with rich nations like the United States. In 1967 the EEC was renamed the European Community.

New Members

Denmark, Ireland, and the United Kingdom joined the European Community in 1973; Greece joined in 1981; and Portugal and Spain became members in 1989. In 1990 East Germany was reunited with West Germany and became a member. In 1993 the European Community was renamed the European Union.

△ *High-speed shuttle trains carry passengers and freight through the Channel Tunnel that links the United Kingdom and France.*

▽ *Increasing cooperation among West European nations has led to the building of jumbo jets called airbuses.*

The Berlin Wall

At the end of World War II, Berlin, Germany's capital, was divided by the victorious Allies into four zones. These later became two zones: Communist East Berlin and non-Communist West Berlin. The East German government built a wall between the two zones to stop people fleeing into West Berlin. In 1989 the East German people rebelled against the Communist regime and joyfully smashed down the wall. In 1990 East and West Germany were reunited as a single state.

△ Portuguese vineyards have been greatly improved with funds made available from the Common Agricultural Policy (CAP). The purpose of this policy is to support agricultural production, but it is also the most important symbol of cooperation between the countries of the European Union (EU). More money is spent on the CAP than on any other EU policy.

The European Union

- Present members with joining dates
- Countries applying to join with possible joining dates
- Possible future applicants
- Non-members

NORWAY (1996)
SWEDEN (1996)
FINLAND (1996)
ESTONIA
RUSSIAN FEDERATION
LATVIA
IRELAND (1973)
UNITED KINGDOM (1973)
DENMARK (1973)
RUSSIAN FEDERATION
LITHUANIA
BELARUS
NETHERLANDS (1958)
GERMANY (1958)
POLAND
•Brussels
BELGIUM (1958)
LUXEMBOURG (1958)
Luxembourg
CZECH REP.
UKRAINE
SLOVAKIA
Strasbourg
FRANCE (1958)
SWITZERLAND
AUSTRIA (1996)
HUNGARY
MOLDOVA
SLOVENIA
CROATIA
ROMANIA
PORTUGAL (1986)
SPAIN (1986)
ITALY (1958)
BOSNIA & HERCEGOVINA
YUGOSLAVIA
BULGARIA
ALBANIA MACEDONIA
TURKEY
GREECE (1981)
MALTA
CYPRUS

▽ The European Union's headquarters are in Brussels, Belgium.

The Future

Other countries, including Austria, Finland, Iceland, Norway, and Sweden, applied for membership in the early 1990's. The European Union is likely to expand even more in the 1990's because several countries in Eastern Europe that dropped their Communist policies in the late 1980's and early 1990's would also like to join.

21

Northern Eurasia

ASIA, the world's largest continent, is joined to Europe. The border between them that follows the Ural Mountains is one of the richest sources of metals in the world. It was a prime source of gold for the ancient Greeks. The border following the Caucasus Mountains between the Caspian and Black Seas has been fought over for thousands of years. It is said that 72 languages were once spoken in the region.

The map shows part of Europe in the west, with northern Asia in the east. This huge region is called Northern Eurasia. It includes the Russian Federation, or Russia, the world's largest country. About a quarter of Russia is in Europe and three-quarters is in Asia.

The 12 countries in Northern Eurasia were once part of the Soviet Union. They became separate countries when the Soviet Union broke up in 1991.

▽ *Samarkand was a center of Islamic culture for several centuries. Its beautiful mosques are now major tourist attractions.*

△ *St. Basil's Cathedral, facing Red Square in the heart of Moscow, was a museum under Communist rule. Christian services can now be held in the church.*

▷ *The boundary between Asia and Europe is shown on the map by broken white lines. It runs from the Arctic Ocean to the Caspian Sea and between the Caspian Sea and the Black Sea.*

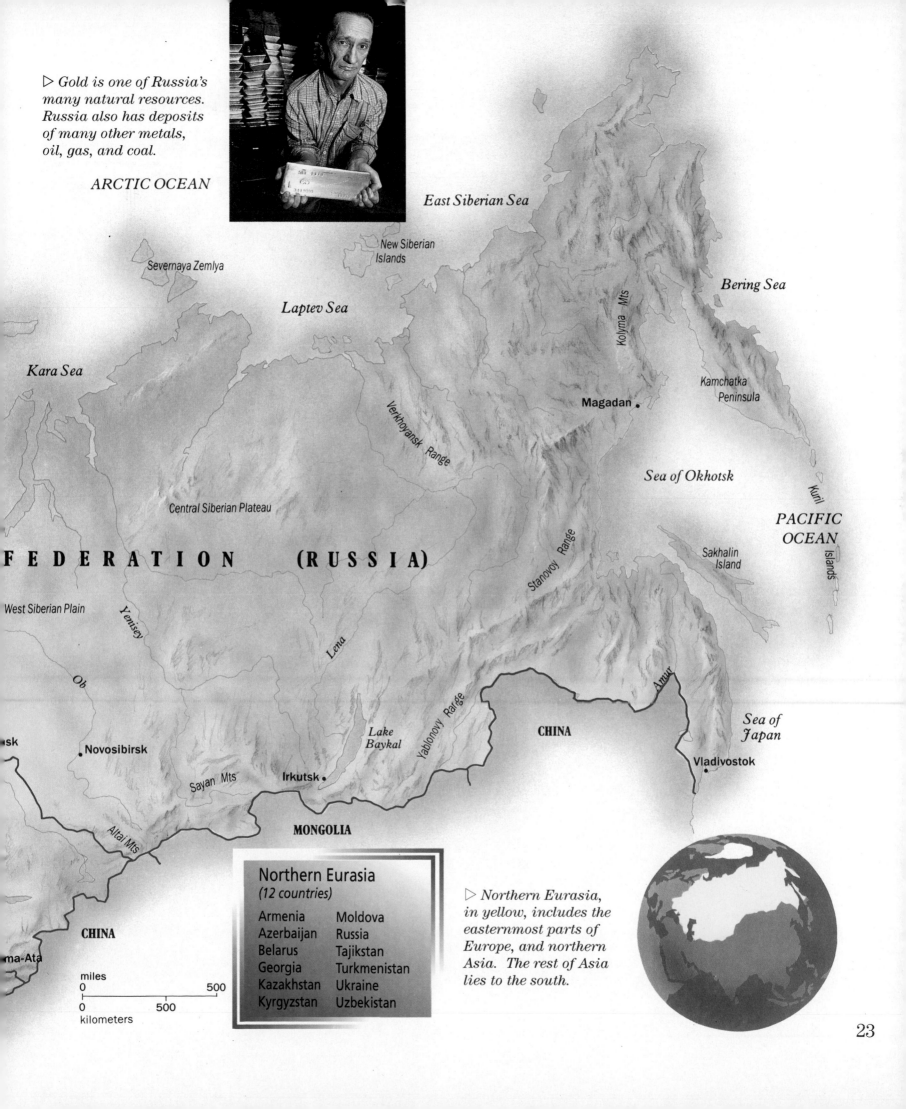

▷ Gold is one of Russia's many natural resources. Russia also has deposits of many other metals, oil, gas, and coal.

ARCTIC OCEAN

East Siberian Sea

New Siberian Islands

Severnaya Zemlya

Laptev Sea

Bering Sea

Kara Sea

Kolyma Mts

Kamchatka Peninsula

Magadan •

Verkhoyansk Range

Sea of Okhotsk

PACIFIC OCEAN

Central Siberian Plateau

Stanovoy Range

Sakhalin Island

Kuril Islands

F E D E R A T I O N   (R U S S I A)

West Siberian Plain

Yenisey

Lena

Amur

Sea of Japan

Ob

Yablonovy Range

CHINA

Vladivostok •

-sk

Novosibirsk •

Lake Baykal

Sayan Mts

Irkutsk •

Altai Mts

MONGOLIA

CHINA

ma-Ata

Northern Eurasia
(12 countries)

Armenia	Moldova
Azerbaijan	Russia
Belarus	Tajikistan
Georgia	Turkmenistan
Kazakhstan	Ukraine
Kyrgyzstan	Uzbekistan

miles
0   500

0   500
kilometers

▷ Northern Eurasia, in yellow, includes the easternmost parts of Europe, and northern Asia. The rest of Asia lies to the south.

SOUTHERN ASIA

SOUTHERN ASIA has more people than any other part of the world. It includes China and India, which have more people than any other countries. In area, they are the fourth and seventh largest countries in the world.

Southern Asia also has some small countries, such as the Maldives, an island nation off the southwest coast of India; Singapore, an island nation in southeastern Asia; and Bahrain, in southwestern Asia.

Asia has many ancient traditions. Farming probably began in southwestern Asia and the earliest civilizations developed in the valleys of the Tigris and Euphrates rivers in what is now Iraq. Other civilizations developed later in the Indus Valley in India and in the Huang He and Chang Jiang Valleys in eastern China.

Religions
Asia was also the birthplace of the world's major religions, including Buddhism, Christianity, Judaism, (Continued on page 26)

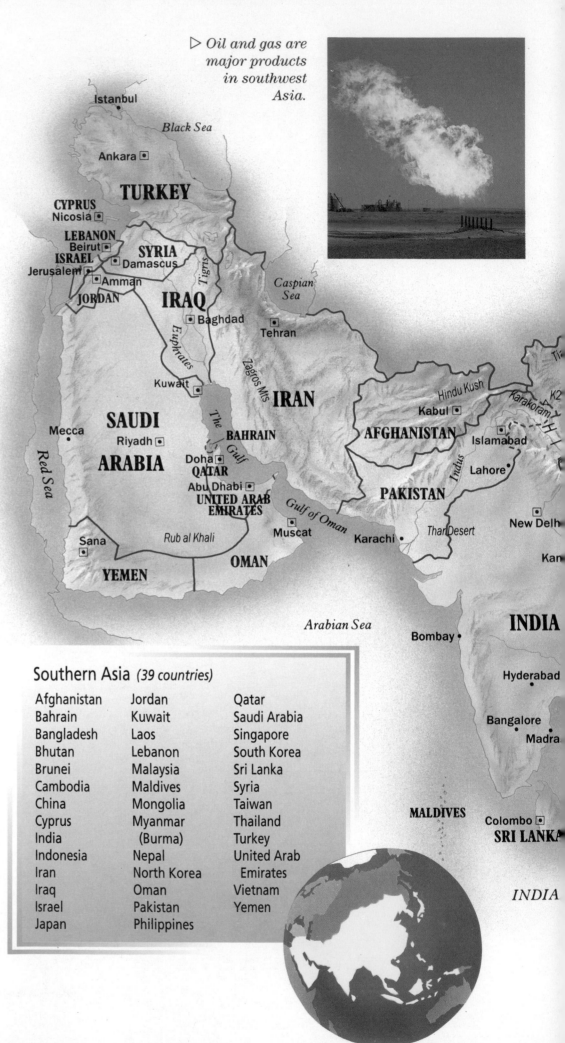

▷ Oil and gas are major products in southwest Asia.

△ Rice is the leading food crop in south-central, southeastern, and eastern Asia. Rice grows in warm, wet climates, as here in Sri Lanka.

Southern Asia (39 countries)

Afghanistan	Jordan	Qatar
Bahrain	Kuwait	Saudi Arabia
Bangladesh	Laos	Singapore
Bhutan	Lebanon	South Korea
Brunei	Malaysia	Sri Lanka
Cambodia	Maldives	Syria
China	Mongolia	Taiwan
Cyprus	Myanmar	Thailand
India	(Burma)	Turkey
Indonesia	Nepal	United Arab
Iran	North Korea	Emirates
Iraq	Oman	Vietnam
Israel	Pakistan	Yemen
Japan	Philippines	

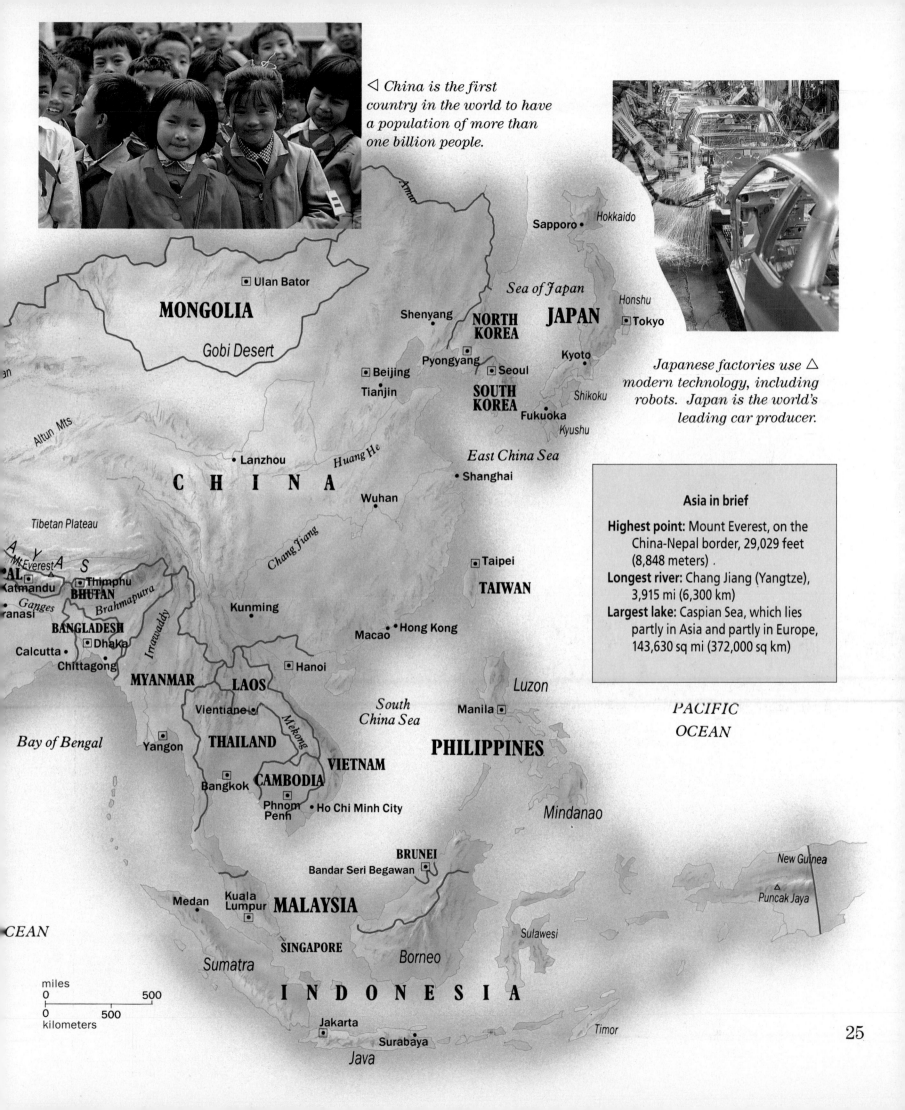

◁ *China is the first country in the world to have a population of more than one billion people.*

Sapporo • Hokkaido

Sea of Japan

Shenyang **NORTH KOREA** **JAPAN** *Honshu*
  • □ Tokyo

Pyongyang □ Kyoto

□ Beijing □ Seoul *Shikoku*

Tianjin **SOUTH KOREA**

Fukuoka •

Kyushu

East China Sea

□ Ulan Bator

MONGOLIA

Gobi Desert

• Lanzhou *Huang He*

C H I N A

Wuhan • • Shanghai

Japanese factories use △ modern technology, including robots. Japan is the world's leading car producer.

Tibetan Plateau

Chang Jiang

□ Taipei

TAIWAN

Kunming •

Asia in brief

Highest point: Mount Everest, on the China-Nepal border, 29,029 feet (8,848 meters) .
Longest river: Chang Jiang (Yangtze), 3,915 mi (6,300 km)
Largest lake: Caspian Sea, which lies partly in Asia and partly in Europe, 143,630 sq mi (372,000 sq km)

A Y A S
A•Mt Everest A S
AL □
atmandu □ •□ Thimphu
Ganges **BHUTAN**
anasi *Brahmaputra*

BANGLADESH
□ Dhaka

Calcutta •

Chittagong •

MYANMAR **LAOS**

Macao • • Hong Kong

Luzon

Vientiane •□ Manila □

Bay of Bengal

Irrawaddy

Yangon • **THAILAND**

Mekong

South China Sea

PHILIPPINES

PACIFIC OCEAN

VIETNAM

Bangkok • **CAMBODIA**

Phnom □
Penh • Ho Chi Minh City

Mindanao

BRUNEI

Bandar Seri Begawan •□

New Guinea

△ *Puncak Jaya*

Medan • Kuala Lumpur □ **MALAYSIA**

CEAN

SINGAPORE *Borneo*

Sulawesi

Sumatra

I N D O N E S I A

miles
0   500
0   500
kilometers

Jakarta □
• Surabaya *Timor*

Java

25

Confucianism, Hinduism, and Islam. Shinto is an important religion in Japan.

The Land and Climate

The land of Asia is the most varied in the world. It has many mountain ranges, including the world's highest, the Himalayas. The

Conflict in the Middle East

Arabs and Israeli Jews have fought over the Golan Heights, the Gaza Strip, and the River Jordan's West Bank since 1948, when modern Israel was created. Holy to Jews, Muslims, and Christians, Jerusalem is capital of Israel, and its Dome of the Rock, below, is one of Islam's holiest shrines. In 1994 Israel took the first steps to peace by withdrawing from some of the Arab-claimed lands.

Himalayas contain Mount Everest, which at 29,029 feet (8,848 meters) is the world's highest peak.

Asia also has many lowlands, especially in the north, where evergreen forests cover large areas on the thinly populated plains and low plateaus of Russia. Southern Asia also has vast lowlands in the south and east, where enormous numbers of people live.

The climate varies greatly. The far north lies in the Arctic region. It has a bitterly cold climate, with long winters. Southern Asia lies near the Equator. This region along with south-central and southeastern Asia is hot and wet.

▷ *The Taj Mahal, in northern India, is the country's best-known building. It is a tomb built by an Indian ruler, Shah Jehan, in memory of his wife, Mumtaz Mahal. Both of their bodies are buried here.*

Hot deserts cover large areas in southwestern Asia.

Cold deserts, such as the Gobi Desert in Mongolia, are found in the interior. The Tibetan plateau, north of the Himalayas, is one of the bleakest places on Earth.

The People

Asia has a great variety of people, including Muslim Turks and Arabs in the southwest, Hindu Indians in south-central Asia, and Chinese and Japanese in the east. A huge number of languages are spoken

in Asia. India alone has 14 major languages, plus about 1,000 minor languages and dialects.

Religious, political, and other differences have led to conflict between peoples. For example, the Jewish people of Israel have fought wars with Arab nations to preserve their country. In southern Asia, conflict between Hindus and Muslims has led to much fighting between India and Pakistan.

Asia contains one of the world's greatest industrial powers. This is Japan, which is one of the world's most prosperous countries. In 1991, 77 percent of Japanese

people lived in cities and towns. By contrast, only 27 percent of the people in India live in cities and towns. Even though India has some of the world's largest cities, including Bombay, Calcutta, and Delhi, most Indians are poor farmers who grow little more than what they need to feed their families.

The poorest countries in Asia are Bhutan and Nepal, which lie north of India. Bangladesh, Laos, and India also rank among the world's 20 poorest countries.

△ *Lamaist monks sit outside their temple in Tibet. Tibetans believe in Lamaism, a kind of Buddhism.*

▷ *A high-speed "bullet train" passes Mount Fuji near Tokyo, Japan.*

The Economy

Agriculture employs about 60 percent of all Asians. The main crops vary according to the climate. The chief food crop in warm, wet regions is rice. The world's top five rice producers — China, India, Indonesia, Bangladesh, and Thailand — account for 75 percent of world production.

In cooler regions, including northern China and Russia, the chief food crop is wheat. Other major farm products include cotton, rubber, sugar, and tea.

Asia has many resources. The nations in southwestern Asia, including Saudi Arabia, Iran, Iraq, and Kuwait, contain about two-thirds of the world's known oil reserves. Several countries in Asia also have large amounts of coal and many metals.

Japan is one of the world's most advanced industrial countries. Other fast-developing areas include South Korea, Hong Kong, Malaysia, and Singapore. Russia also has many industries, and the number of factories in China and India is growing rapidly. Tourism is also important in many Asian countries.

Hong Kong

Hong Kong has one of the world's busiest ports, and is the tenth biggest trading nation in the world even though it is only 413 sq mi (1,070 sq km) in area. It is renowned for manufacturing textiles, clothing, cameras, and electrical goods. Hong Kong, a British colony since 1842, will return to Chinese control in 1997.

◁ *Malaysia produces about a quarter of the world's natural rubber. Rubber is made from latex, a white juice that comes from the rubber tree.*

27

AFRICA

AFRICA is the second largest continent after Asia. It covers about a fifth of the world's land area. The continent contains 53 independent countries. At the end of World War II in 1945, most of these countries were colonies, ruled by Britain, France, Portugal, and Spain.

Africa (53 countries)

Algeria	Central African	Eritrea	Kenya	Nigeria
Angola	Republic	Ethiopia	Lesotho	Rwanda
Benin	Chad	Gabon	Liberia	São Tomé &
Botswana	Comoros	Gambia	Libya	Principe
Burkina Faso	Congo	Ghana	Madagascar	Senegal
Burundi	Djibouti	Guinea	Malawi	Seychelles
Cameroon	Egypt	Guinea-Bissau	Mali	Sierra Leone
Cape Verde	Equatorial Guinea	Ivory Coast	Mauritania	Somali Republic
			Mauritius	South Africa
			Morocco	Sudan
			Mozambique	Swaziland
			Namibia	Tanzania
			Niger	Togo
				Tunisia
				Uganda
				Zaire
				Zambia
				Zimbabwe

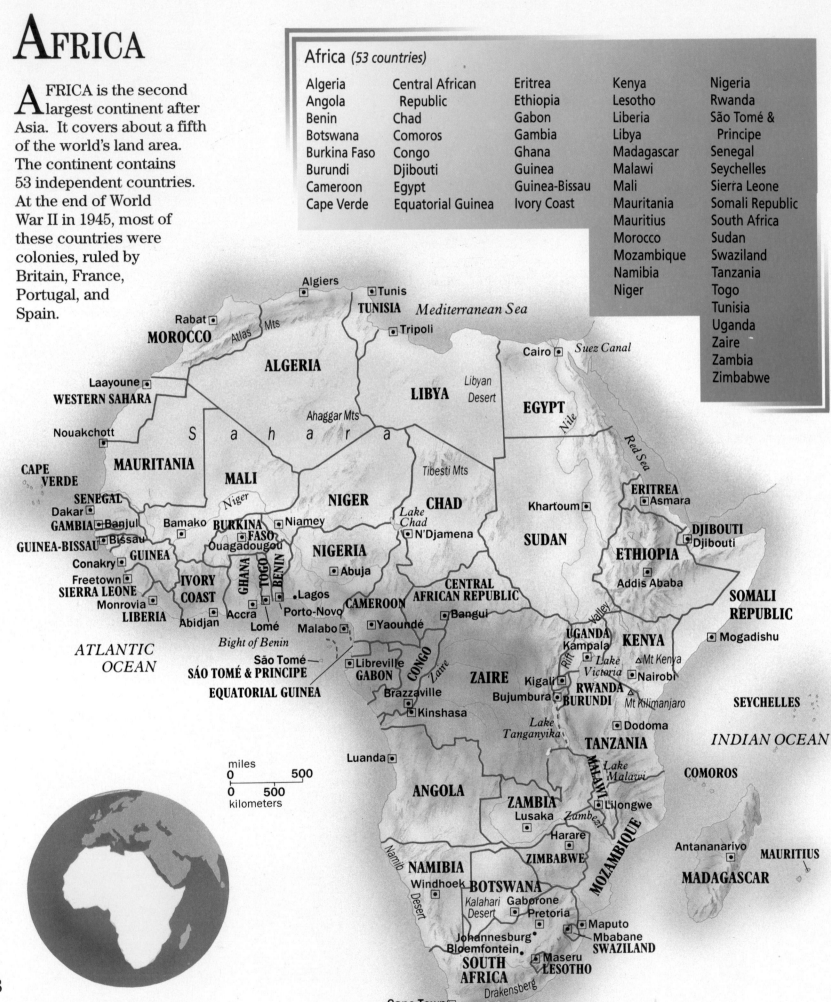

28

The Land

A huge plateau surrounded by narrow coastal plains makes up much of Africa. In the east a deep valley cuts through the plateau. Great rivers, including the Nile, Zaire, and Niger, drain the plateau.

Mountain ranges rise in northwestern and southern Africa. The highest peaks, such as Kilimanjaro, are old volcanoes. Africa includes several islands. Madagascar, off the southeast coast, is the world's fourth largest island.

The Climate

The Equator runs through the middle of Africa and most of the continent is hot or warm throughout the year. But the highlands are much cooler than the steamy coastlands.

Africa has huge deserts, including the Sahara, the world's largest, in the north, and the Namib and Kalahari deserts in the south. Vast rain forests grow near the Equator, where the rainfall is heavy. Between the forests and the deserts are grasslands, where such animals as elephants, lions,

▷ *The pyramids of Egypt were built around 4,500 years ago. Ancient Egypt was the first great civilization.*

and zebras are found.

The climate is mild in the far northwest and southwest of Africa, with hot, dry summers and mild, rainy winters.

The People and the Economy

Most of the people in northern Africa are Arabs or Berbers, who speak Arabic and follow Islam. Black Africans live south of the Sahara, where more than 1,000 languages are spoken. Some Black Africans are Christians and others are Muslims, but many follow old African religions.

Africa has some rich resources, such as oil and gas in the north, and gold and diamonds in the

south. But most Africans are farmers. Living standards are generally lower than in other continents. Severe droughts may cause many people to starve.

Africa in brief

Highest point: Kilimanjaro, in Tanzania, 19,340 feet (5,895 meters)
Longest river: Nile, 4,415 mi (6,671 km)
Largest lake: Victoria, 26,828 sq mi (69,484 sq km)

▽ *Farmers grow food to feed their families. Spare produce is sold in local markets.*

▽ *Warm grasslands lie at the foot of Africa's highest peak, the snow-capped Kilimanjaro in Tanzania.*

AUSTRALIA AND THE PACIFIC

AUSTRALIA is the only country that is also a continent. Australia, with Papua New Guinea, New Zealand, and other nearby islands, forms a region called Australasia. Australasia, with the many small Pacific islands lying to the east and north, forms a region known as Oceania.

The first, or Aboriginal, people of Australia probably came to the continent from Asia more than 50,000 years ago. But most Australians today are descendants of Europeans. Australia has huge cattle and sheep farms. Farm products include fruits, sugarcane, and wheat.

Australia
Australia is a mostly dry and flat continent. The only large mountain ranges are in the east. The east also has most of the best farmland. Much of western Australia is desert.

Australia in brief

Highest point: Mount Kosciusko, in the southeast, 7,310 feet (2,228 meters)
Longest river: Darling, 1,702 mi (2,739 km)
Largest lake: Lake Eyre*, 3,700 sq mi (9,583 sq km)

*contains water only after heavy rains

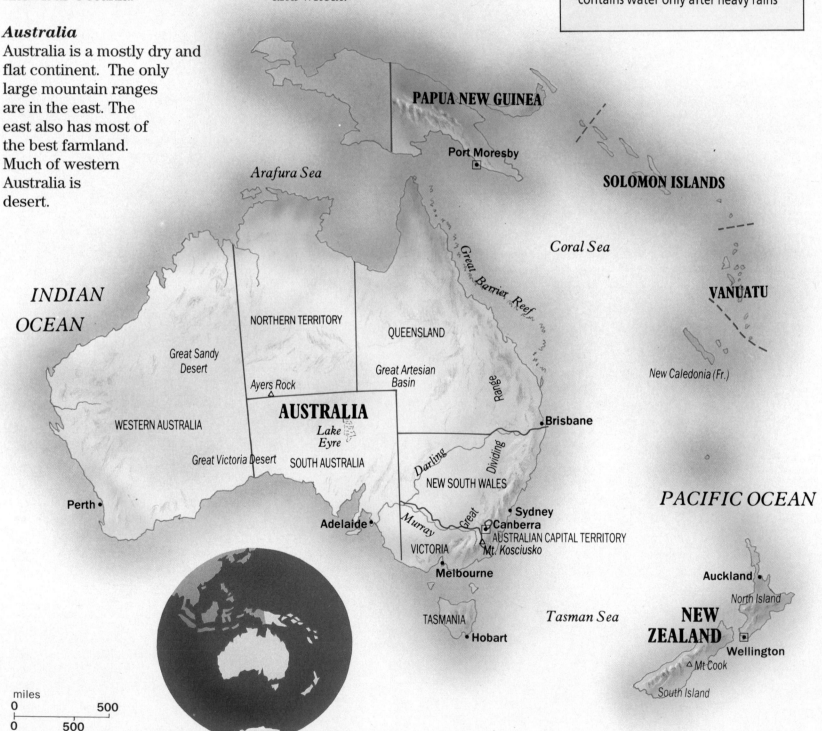

PAPUA NEW GUINEA

Port Moresby

Arafura Sea

SOLOMON ISLANDS

Coral Sea

INDIAN OCEAN

VANUATU

NORTHERN TERRITORY

QUEENSLAND

Great Sandy Desert

Great Barrier Reef

Great Artesian Basin

New Caledonia (Fr.)

Ayers Rock

AUSTRALIA

Range

Lake Eyre

WESTERN AUSTRALIA

Great Victoria Desert

SOUTH AUSTRALIA

Brisbane

Darling

Dividing

Perth

NEW SOUTH WALES

PACIFIC OCEAN

Adelaide

Murray

Great

Sydney
Canberra
AUSTRALIAN CAPITAL TERRITORY
Mt. Kosciusko

VICTORIA

Auckland

Melbourne

North Island

TASMANIA

Tasman Sea

NEW ZEALAND

Hobart

Wellington

Mt Cook

South Island

miles
0   500
0   500
kilometers

30

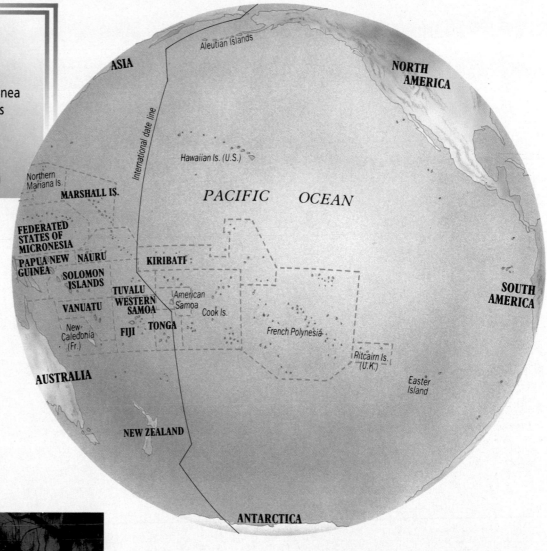

New Zealand

North Island, New Zealand, is warm and has several volcanoes. South Island is cooler and mountainous.

The first known people to settle in New Zealand came from the Polynesian islands to the east. These people are called the Maoris. But most New Zealanders today are descendants of British settlers. New Zealand is famous for its farm products, including butter, cheese, meat, and wool. Forestry is also an important industry.

◁ *Ayers Rock is a famous landmark in the heart of Australia.*

▷ *Melanesians live in Papua New Guinea, north of Australia.*

The Pacific Islands

There are three main groups of Pacific islands: Melanesia, Micronesia, and Polynesia. Melanesia means "black islands." This refers to the dark skins of the people. Melanesia includes Papua New Guinea, the Solomon Islands, New Caledonia, Fiji, and Vanuatu. Micronesia means "tiny islands." This region includes the Marshall Islands, the Federated States of Micronesia, and Nauru.

Polynesia means "many islands." This group of islands sprawls across a huge area and includes Tonga, Western Samoa, Kiribati, and French Polynesia. The U.S. state of Hawaii, in the north, is also part of Polynesia, as is Easter Island, a Chilean territory in the east.

31

THE HUMAN WORLD

HUMAN ACTIVITIES, such as farming and the building of cities, industries, and roads, have changed the appearance of many parts of the world.

Farming

Farming is the world's most important industry. It supplies food and other items used for clothing and shelter, which everyone needs.

Crop farming is limited to only about

a tenth of the world's land area, while another fifth is used for pastoral, or animal, farming. The rest of the world's land area is too cold, too dry, or too rugged for farming. Few people live in these areas.

People first began to grow crops about 11,000 years ago in the Middle East. As food became plentiful, some people gave up farming and moved to settlements where they worked in new craft industries. This change in human society was the first step toward the development of civilizations.

Cities

The earliest cities were founded about 5,500 years ago. Today, most people in the richer, developed countries live in cities and towns, but most people in poorer, developing countries still live in rural areas.

For example, 75 percent of the people in the United States live in urban areas. By contrast, in India, 73 percent of the people live in rural areas. Many Indians are poor farmers who produce little

more than what they need to look after their families.

Many city people are employed in manufacturing industries. But in many cities, even larger

△ *Manufacturing microchips takes great care. They become the "brains" of computers and robots, which are replacing people in many jobs.*

◁ *The world's growing population is a heavy burden on the Earth's resources. In poorer countries like India (left) many children die of starvation. Governments must work hard to improve living conditions and provide better education for the poor.*

Human activities map key

	Cereal grains
	Rice
	Mostly uncultivated
🍎	Fruit
🐄	Cattle
🐑	Sheep
	Most populated areas
	Most populated areas in cereal growing regions
	Most populated areas in rice growing regions
★	Cities above 10 million people
▪	Cities above 5 million people

Pastoral Farming

Pastoral land, where farm animals are raised, covers about a fifth of the world's land area. Animals are usually kept on land that is unsuitable for crops. Sheep rearing is important in New Zealand, right, which has about 20 times as many farm animals as people.

than rural people. But city life also includes overcrowding, crime, and pollution. Human progress has had a major impact on our world, causing great destruction of nature in many areas.

▽ *The overgrazing of grasslands in central Chad, Africa, has turned once fertile areas into desert. Here, herdsmen draw water from a well.*

numbers work in service industries, such as government, health, finance, or education. In the United States, the world's richest country, farming and manufacturing are highly efficient. By the early 1990's, farming employed only 3 percent of the U.S. labor force, while industry employed 26 percent.

It costs more to live in cities than in rural areas. City people often enjoy better services, including hospitals and schools,

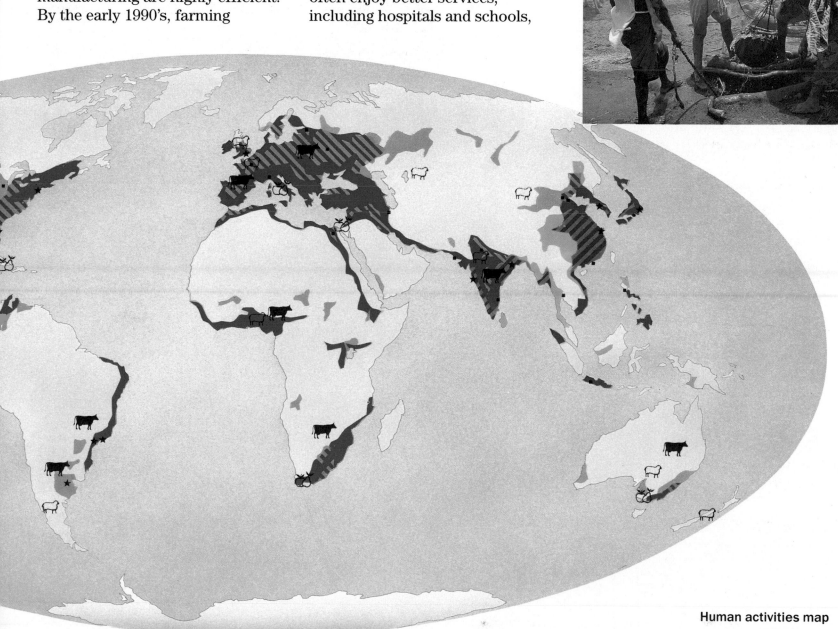

Human activities map

CLIMATE

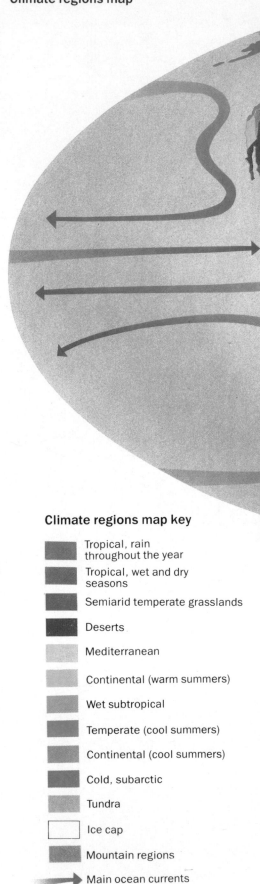

THE CLIMATE of an area is its usual, or average, weather. Part of a desert may have heavy rainstorms every few years. But if its average rainfall is less than 10 inches (250 millimeters) per year, then that area is described as a desert.

Climatic Factors

Every place has a different climate, depending on where exactly on the Earth it is. Areas near the Equator are generally warmer than areas near the poles. Mountains affect climate, because highland is colder than nearby lowland. Even on the Equator, snow always covers the highest mountaintops. The summit of Kilimanjaro, in Tanzania, is covered with snow all year long.

Climate is also affected by the ocean currents. For example, the Gulf Stream, which flows from the Gulf of Mexico, warms the climate of northwestern Europe. Places near the sea usually have milder climates than places far inland.

World Climates

Different places around the world can have similar climates. For example, deserts cover huge areas of Africa, Australia, and North America. The climate in

these areas is hot and dry.

The climate in continental regions is neither very hot nor very cold. In warm continental regions around the Mediterranean Sea, the summers are long and hot and the winters cool and wet. Cool continental climates, found in much of Europe, Russia, and North America, have cooler summers and snowy winters.

In the tropical regions, on either side of the Equator, the kind of land determines the climate. Rain forest areas have rain throughout the year, and tropical grasslands have a marked dry season.

The coldest parts of the Earth are the regions around the North and South Poles. The climate in these places is very harsh, with temperatures well below the freezing point most of the year, and snow and ice covering the ground. Even during the summer, when it is always light at the poles, the Sun cannot melt the ice caps.

△ Northern England has a cool temperate climate.

◁ The Sahara is the world's largest desert. Parts of it are covered by huge hills of sand called dunes. Desert people travel from place to place to find water for themselves and their animals.

Climate regions map key

- Tropical, rain throughout the year
- Tropical, wet and dry seasons
- Semiarid temperate grasslands
- Deserts
- Mediterranean
- Continental (warm summers)
- Wet subtropical
- Temperate (cool summers)
- Continental (cool summers)
- Cold, subarctic
- Tundra
- Ice cap
- Mountain regions
- Main ocean currents

▷ The maps show the average January and July temperatures throughout the world. Temperatures and rainfall are the two main factors that determine the climate of any area.

▽ The map shows the average yearly rainfall in different parts of the world.

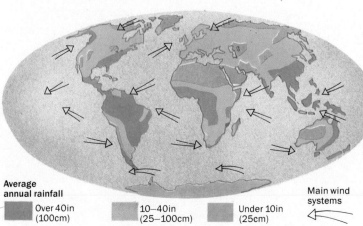

World average temperatures

°C	°F
−45	−49
−35	−31
−25	−13
−15	5
−5	23
0	32
5	41
15	59
25	77
30	86
35	95

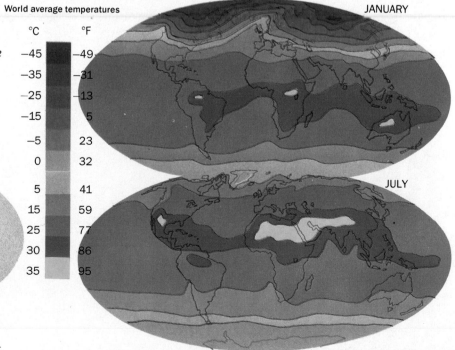

JANUARY

JULY

Average annual rainfall

Over 40in (100cm) 10–40in (25–100cm) Under 10in (25cm)

Main wind systems ⟵

THE ENVIRONMENT: POLLUTION OF LAND, SEA, AND ATMOSPHERE

IN THE LAST 200 YEARS the damage that people have done to the environment has increased dramatically. This is partly due to the building of large industrial cities and partly because of the growth in the world's population from about 1.2 billion in 1850 to more than 5 billion today.

Land Pollution

Soil is often polluted by pesticides, which kill bacteria and other creatures that make the soil fertile.

Cutting down forests and overgrazing or over-farming land removes the protective cover of grass and roots on the ground. As a result the soil is often blown away by the wind or washed away by running water. Sometimes fertile areas, such as the dry grasslands south of the Sahara, become deserts.

Water Pollution

Some factories dump poisonous waste in rivers, killing living things and endangering people. Some factory waste reaches the sea and pollutes coastal waters. At sea, damaged oil tankers sometimes spill great amounts of oil, which destroys marine life.

Air Pollution

Factories, power stations, and cars produce poisonous gases that cause smog. These gases contain

Land and sea pollution map key

- Existing desert
- Areas at risk from desertification
- Tropical rain forest
- Rain forest seriously damaged in recent years
- The most polluted seas
- The most polluted rivers
- Sites of known nuclear accidents

Rain forest destruction

Rain forests contain more than half the world's plants and animals and produce much of the oxygen we breathe. Their destruction is seriously harmful to our planet.

Air pollution map

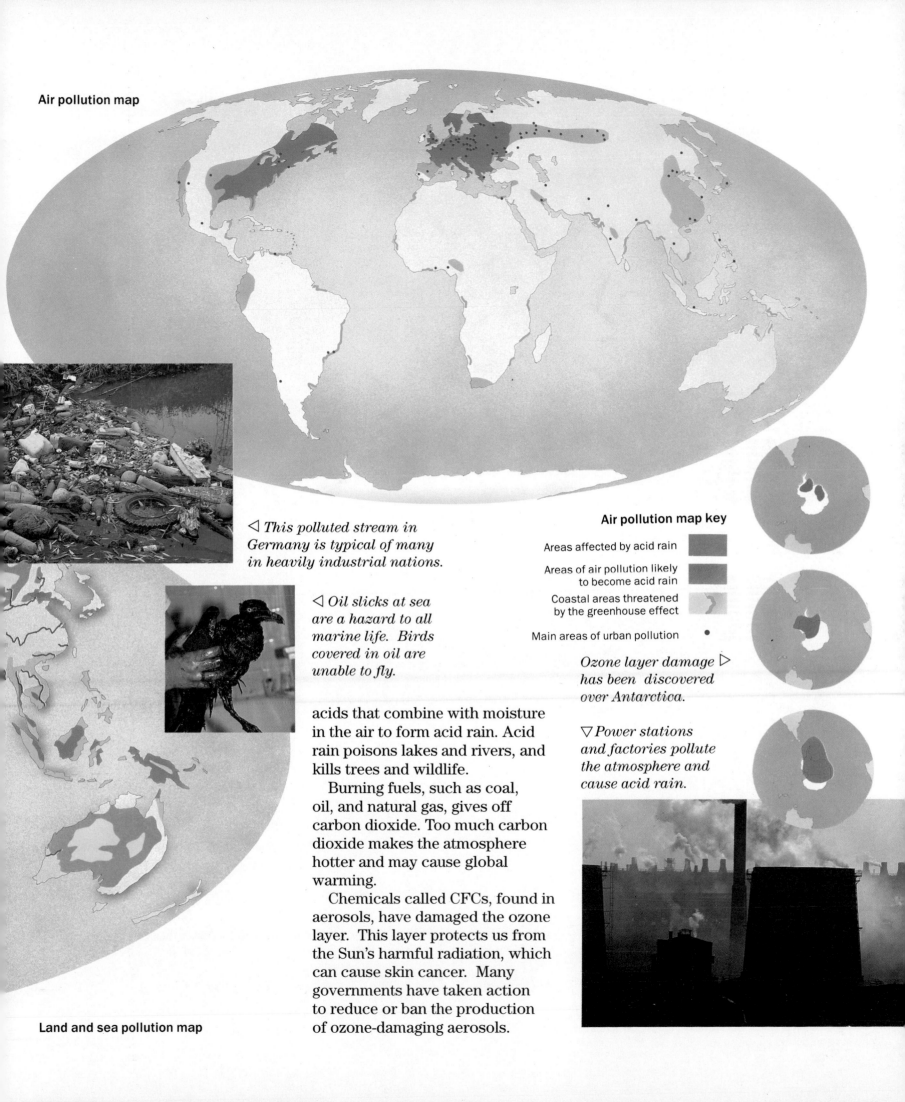

◁ *This polluted stream in Germany is typical of many in heavily industrial nations.*

◁ *Oil slicks at sea are a hazard to all marine life. Birds covered in oil are unable to fly.*

Air pollution map key

Areas affected by acid rain

Areas of air pollution likely to become acid rain

Coastal areas threatened by the greenhouse effect

Main areas of urban pollution

Ozone layer damage ▷ has been discovered over Antarctica.

acids that combine with moisture in the air to form acid rain. Acid rain poisons lakes and rivers, and kills trees and wildlife.

Burning fuels, such as coal, oil, and natural gas, gives off carbon dioxide. Too much carbon dioxide makes the atmosphere hotter and may cause global warming.

Chemicals called CFCs, found in aerosols, have damaged the ozone layer. This layer protects us from the Sun's harmful radiation, which can cause skin cancer. Many governments have taken action to reduce or ban the production of ozone-damaging aerosols.

▽ *Power stations and factories pollute the atmosphere and cause acid rain.*

Land and sea pollution map

WORLD INFORMATION TABLE: INDEPENDENT COUNTRIES

p. – page numbers refer to location on main continental maps

p.	Country	Area sq mi	Area sq km	Population	Capital
24	Afghanistan	251,773	652,090	21,558,000	Kabul
17	Albania	11,100	28,748	3,338,000	Tiranë
28	Algeria	919,595	2,381,741	26,375,000	Algiers
17	Andorra	175	453	60,000	Andorra la Vella
28	Angola	481,354	1,246,700	9,732,000	Luanda
15	Antigua & Barbuda	170	440	81,000	St. John's
15	Argentina	1,068,302	2,776,889	33,099,000	Buenos Aires
22	Armenia	11,506	29,800	3,499,000	Yerevan
30	Australia	2,978,147	7,713,364	17,540,000	Canberra
17	Austria	32,376	83,853	7,906,000	Vienna
22	Azerbaijan	33,436	86,600	7,145,000	Baku
15	Bahamas	5,358	13,878	263,000	Nassau
24	Bahrain	262	678	532,000	Manama
25	Bangladesh	55,598	143,998	112,832,000	Dhaka
15	Barbados	166	430	259,000	Bridgetown
22	Belarus	80,155	207,600	10,346,000	Minsk
17	Belgium	11,783	30,519	10,039,000	Brussels
15	Belize	8,867	22,965	200,000	Belmopan
28	Benin	43,484	112,622	5,042,000	Porto-Novo
25	Bhutan	18,147	47,000	1,497,000	Thimphu
15	Bolivia	424,165	1,098,581	7,527,000	La Paz
17	Bosnia & Hercegovina	19,741	51,129	4,383,000	Sarajevo
28	Botswana	224,607	581,730	1,360,000	Garborone
15	Brazil	3,286,488	8,511,965	153,850,000	Brasilia
25	Brunei	2,226	5,765	273,000	Bandar Seri Begawan
17	Bulgaria	42,823	110,912	8,952,000	Sofia
28	Burkina Faso	105,792	274,000	9,537,000	Ouagadougou
28	Burundi	10,747	27,834	5,818,000	Bujumbura
25	Cambodia	69,898	181,035	9,010,000	Phnom Penh
28	Cameroon	183,569	475,442	12,245,000	Yaoundé
8-9	Canada	3,851,809	9,976,139	27,344,000	Ottawa
28	Cape Verde	1,557	4,033	389,000	Praia
28	Central African Republic	240,535	622,984	3,166,000	Bangui
28	Chad	495,755	1,284,000	5,977,000	N'Djamena
15	Chile	292,258	756,945	13,599,000	Santiago
25	China	3,705,408	9,596,961	1,166,144,000	Beijing
15	Colombia	439,737	1,138,914	33,405,000	Bogotá
28	Comoros	863	2,235	510,000	Moroni
28	Congo	132,047	342,000	2,428,000	Brazzaville
15	Costa Rica	19,730	51,100	3,135,000	San José
17	Croatia	21,829	56,538	4,773,000	Zagreb
15	Cuba	42,804	110,861	10,841,000	Havana
24	Cyprus	3,572	9,251	715,000	Nicosia
17,19	Czech Republic	30,441	78,841	10,383,000	Prague
17	Denmark	16,632	43,077	5,166,000	Copenhagen
28	Djibouti	8,958	23,200	465,000	Djibouti
15	Dominica	290	751	72,000	Roseau
15	Dominican Republic	18,816	48,734	7,321,000	Santo Domingo
15	Ecuador	109,484	283,561	11,028,000	Quito
28	Egypt	386,662	1,001,449	54,805,000	Cairo
15	El Salvador	8,124	21,041	5,389,000	San Salvador
28	Equatorial Guinea	10,831	28,051	437,000	Malabo
28	Eritrea	45,406	117,600	3,318,000	Asmara
17	Estonia	17,413	45,100	1,554,000	Tallinn
28	Ethiopia	426,373	1,104,300	50,527,000	Addis Ababa
31	Fiji	7,056	18,274	750,000	Suva
17	Finland	130,559	338,145	5,062,000	Helsinki
17	France	212,935	551,500	57,338,000	Paris
28	Gabon	103,347	267,667	1,201,000	Libreville
28	Gambia	4,361	11,295	929,000	Banjul
22	Georgia	26,911	69,700	5,493,000	Tbilisi
17	Germany	137,804	356,910	80,553,000	Berlin
28	Ghana	92,098	238,533	15,824,000	Accra
17	Greece	50,962	131,990	10,454,000	Athens
15	Grenada	133	344	91,000	St. George's
15	Guatemala	42,042	108,889	9,746,000	Guatemala City
28	Guinea	94,926	245,857	6,048,000	Conakry
28	Guinea-Bissau	13,948	36,125	1,002,000	Bissau
15	Guyana	83,000	214,969	806,000	Georgetown
15	Haiti	10,714	27,750	6,715,000	Port-au-Prince
15	Honduras	43,277	112,088	5,418,000	Tegucigalpa
17	Hungary	35,920	93,032	10,202,000	Budapest
17	Iceland	39,769	103,000	261,000	Reykjavik
25	India	1,269,346	3,287,590	883,476,000	New Delhi
25	Indonesia	735,358	1,904,569	184,274,000	Jakarta
24	Iran	636,296	1,648,000	59,791,000	Tehran
24	Iraq	169,235	438,317	19,184,000	Baghdad
17	Ireland	27,137	70,284	3,536,000	Dublin
24	Israel	8,130	21,056	5,113,000	Jerusalem
17	Italy	116,320	301,268	57,844,000	Rome
28	Ivory Coast	124,504	322,463	12,841,000	Abidjan
15	Jamaica	4,243	10,990	2,394,000	Kingston
25	Japan	145,870	377,801	124,318,000	Tokyo
24	Jordan	37,738	97,740	3,949,000	Amman
22	Kazakhstan	1,049,156	2,717,300	16,954,000	Alma-Ata
28	Kenya	224,081	580,367	25,838,000	Nairobi
31	Kiribati	280	726	75,000	Tarawa
24	Kuwait	6,880	17,818	1,400,000	Kuwait
22	Kyrgyzstan	76,641	198,500	4,472,000	Bishkek
25	Laos	91,429	236,800	4,384,000	Vientiane
17	Latvia	24,904	64,500	2,617,000	Riga
24	Lebanon	4,015	10,400	3,781,000	Beirut
28	Lesotho	11,720	30,355	1,860,000	Maseru
28	Liberia	43,000	111,369	2,719,000	Monrovia
28	Libya	679,362	1,759,540	4,873,000	Tripoli
17	Liechtenstein	62	160	30,000	Vaduz
17	Lithuania	25,174	65,200	3,754,000	Vilnius
17	Luxembourg	998	2,586	389,000	Luxembourg
17	Macedonia	9,928	25,713	2,172,000	Skopje
28	Madagascar	226,658	587,041	12,384,000	Antananarivo
28	Malawi	45,747	118,484	9,085,000	Lilongwe
25	Malaysia	127,317	329,749	18,610,000	Kuala Lumpur
24	Maldives	115	298	228,000	Male
28	Mali	478,841	1,240,192	8,962,000	Bamako
17	Malta	122	316	36,000	Valletta
31	Marshall Islands	70	181	50,000	Majuro
28	Mauritania	395,956	1,025,520	2,082,000	Nouakchott
28	Mauritius	720	1,865	1,099,000	Port Louis
15	Mexico	756,066	1,958,201	84,967,000	Mexico City
31	Micronesia, Federated States of	271	702	108,000	Palikir
22	Moldova	13,012	33,700	4,359,000	Chisinau
17	Monaco	0.7	1.9	30,000	Monaco
25	Mongolia	604,829	1,566,500	2,311,000	Ulan Bator
28	Morocco	172,414	446,550	26,262,000	Rabat
28	Mozambique	309,496	801,590	16,565,000	Maputo
25	Myanmar (Burma)	261,228	676,578	43,718,000	Yangon (Rangoon)
28	Namibia	318,261	824,292	1,529,000	Windhoek
31	Nauru	8	21	9,000	——
25	Nepal	54,362	140,797	19,892,000	Katmandu
17	Netherlands	15,770	40,844	15,167,000	Amsterdam
30	New Zealand	104,628	207,986	3,415,000	Wellington
15	Nicaragua	50,193	130,000	3,916,000	Managua
28	Niger	489,191	1,267,000	8,171,000	Niamey
28	Nigeria	356,669	923,768	101,884,000	Abuja

p.	Country	Area sq mi	Area sq km	Population	Capital
25	North Korea	46,474	120,538	22,614,000	Pyongyang
17	Norway	125,057	323,895	4,281,000	Oslo
24	Oman	82,030	212,457	1,647,000	Muscat
24	Pakistan	307,374	796,095	119,347,000	Islamabad
15	Panama	29,157	75,517	2,514,000	Panama City
30	Papua New Guinea	178,704	462,840	4,055,000	Port Moresby
15	Paraguay	157,048	406,752	4,519,000	Asunción
15	Peru	496,225	1,285,216	22,370,000	Lima
25	Philippines	115,831	300,000	64,189,000	Manila
17	Poland	124,808	323,250	38,365,000	Warsaw
17	Portugal	35,672	92,389	9,843,000	Lisbon
24	Qatar	4,247	11,000	524,000	Doha
17	Romania	91,699	237,500	22,865,000	Bucharest
21-22	Russian Federation	6,592,849	17,075,400	148,920,000	Moscow
28	Rwanda	10,169	26,338	7,310,000	Kigali
15	St. Kitts-Nevis	101	261	42,000	Basseterre
15	St. Lucia	240	622	156,000	Castries
15	St. Vincent & the Grenadines	150	388	104,000	Kingstown
17	San Marino	24	61	24,000	San Marino
28	São Tomé & Principe	372	964	121,000	São Tomé
24	Saudi Arabia	830,000	2,149,690	15,909,000	Riyadh
28	Senegal	75,955	196,722	7,845,000	Dakar
28	Seychelles	176	455	69,000	Victoria
28	Sierra Leone	27,699	71,740	4,354,000	Freetown
25	Singapore	239	618	2,814,000	Singapore
17	Slovakia	18,933	49,035	5,346,000	Bratislava
17	Slovenia	7,819	20,251	2,017,000	Ljubljana
30	Solomon Islands	11,157	28,896	385,000	Honiara
28	Somalia Republic	246,201	637,657	8,302,000	Mogadishu
28	South Africa	471,445	1,221,037	39,763,000	Cape Town; Pretoria; Bloemfontein
25	South Korea	38,230	99,016	43,663,000	Seoul
17	Spain	194,897	504,782	39,077,000	Madrid
24	Sri Lanka	25,332	65,610	17,396,000	Colombo
28	Sudan	976,500	2,505,813	26,587,000	Khartoum
15	Suriname	63,037	168,265	467,000	Paramaribo
28	Swaziland	6,704	17,364	860,000	Mbabane
17	Sweden	173,732	449,964	8,707,000	Stockholm
17	Switzerland	15,943	41,293	6,864,000	Bern
24	Syria	71,498	185,180	12,961,000	Damascus
25	Taiwan	13,900	36,000	20,727,000	Taipei
22	Tajikistan	55,251	143,100	5,634,000	Dushanbe
28	Tanzania	364,900	945,087	25,965,000	Dodoma
25	Thailand	198,115	513,115	57,992,000	Bangkok
28	Togo	21,925	56,785	3,899,000	Lomé
31	Tonga	288	747	101,000	Nukualofa
15	Trinidad & Tobago	1,981	5,130	1,268,000	Port-of-Spain
28	Tunisia	63,170	163,610	8,405,000	Tunis
24	Turkey	300,948	779,452	58,467,000	Ankara
22	Turkmenistan	188,456	488,100	3,852,000	Ashkhabad
31	Tuvalu	10	26	10,000	Fongafale on Funafuti atoll
28	Uganda	91,074	235,880	17,475,000	Kampala
19,22	Ukraine	233,090	603,700	52,118,000	Kiev
24	United Arab Emirates	32,278	83,600	1,668,000	Abu Dhabi
17	United Kingdom	94,248	244,100	57,701,000	London
8,9	United States	3,787,443	9,809,431	255,414,000	Washington, D.C.
15	Uruguay	68,500	177,414	3,131,000	Montevideo
22	Uzbekistan	172,742	447,400	21,285,000	Tashkent
30	Vanatu	4,706	12,189	155,000	Port-Vila
17	Vatican City	0.17	0.44	1,000	—
15	Venezuela	352,145	912,050	20,310,000	Caracas
25	Vietnam	128,066	331,689	69,225,000	Hanoi
31	Western Samoa	1,093	2,831	162,000	Apia
24	Yemen	203,850	527,968	13,128,000	Sana
19	Yugoslavia*	39,449	102,173	10,597,000	Belgrade
28	Zaire	905,355	2,344,858	39,794,000	Kinshasa
28	Zambia	290,587	752,618	8,589,000	Lusaka
28	Zimbabwe	150,873	390,759	10,352,000	Harare

* Consisting of the former Yugoslav republics of Montenegro and Serbia

POPULATED DEPENDENCIES

Australia (A) Chile (C) Denmark (D) France (F) Netherlands (N) New Zealand (N.Z.) Portugal (P)
United Kingdom (U.K.) United States of America (U.S.A.)

p.	Dependency	Area sq mi	Area sq km	Population	Capital
31	American Samoa (U.S.A.)	77	199	39,000	Pago Pago
†	Anguilla (U.K.)	37	96	7,000	The Valley
†	Aruba (N)	75	193	61,000	Oranjestad
†	Azores (P)	905	2,344	250,000	Ponta Delgada
†	Bermuda (U.K.)	20	53	52,000	Hamilton
†	Cayman Is. (U.K.)	100	259	24,000	Georgetown
†	Channel Is. (U.K.)	75	195	147,000	St. Helier; St. Peter Port
31	Cook Is. (N.Z.)	91	236	17,000	Avarua
31	Easter Island (C)	47	122	2,000	—
†	Faeroe Is. (D)	540	1,399	48,000	Tórshavn
15	Falkland Is. (U.K.)	4,700	12,173	2,100	Stanley
15	French Guiana (F)	34,749	90,000	96,000	Cayenne
31	French Polynesia (F)	1,544	4,000	207,000	Papeete
26	Gaza Strip	146	378	658,000	Gaza
17	Gibraltar (U.K.)	2	6	32,000	Gibraltar
6	Greenland (D)	840,004	2,175,600	58,000	Godthab
15	Guadeloupe (F)	658	1,705	400,000	Basse-Terre
†	Guam (U.S.A.)	209	541	150,000	Agana
25	Hong Kong (U.K.)	403	1,045	5,805,000	Victoria
25	Macao (P)	6	16	487,000	Macao
†	Madeira Is. (P)	308	797	253,000	Funchal
†	Man, Isle of (U.K.)	227	588	67,000	Douglas
15	Martinique (F)	425	1,102	366,000	Fort-de-France
†	Midway Island (U.S.A.)	2	5	500	—
†	Montserrat (U.K.)	38	98	12,000	Plymouth
†	Netherlands Antilles (N)	309	800	194,000	Willemstad
30	New Caledonia (F)	7,172	18,575	175,000	Nouméa
†	Niue Island (N.Z.)	100	260	2,500	—
†	Norfolk Island (A)	14	36	2,000	—
31	Northern Mariana Is. (U.S.A.)	184	477	47,000	Saipan
†	Palau, or Belau (U.S.A.) (Also called Trust Territory of the Pacific Islands)	192	497	15,000	Koror
31	Pitcairn Is. Group (U.K.)	2	5	60	—
15	Puerto Rico (U.S.A.)	3,435	8,897	3,554,000	San Juan
†	Réunion (F)	969	2,510	611,000	Saint-Denis
†	St. Helena Group (U.K.)	121	314	7,000	Jamestown
†	St. Pierre & Miquelon (F)	93	242	6,000	St. Pierre
†	Tokelau (N.Z.)	5	12	2,000	—
†	Turks & Caicos Is. (U.K.)	166	430	11,000	Grand Turk
†	Virgin Is. (U.K.)	59	153	17,000	Road Town
†	Virgin Is. (U.S.A.)	132	342	97,000	Charlotte Amalie
†	Wake Island (U.S.A.)	3	8	300	—
†	Wallis & Futuna Is. (F)	77	200	14,000	Mata-Uta
26	West Bank *	2,263	5,860	973,000	
28	Western Sahara **	103,577	266,000	162,000	El Aaiún

† Not shown on map * Claimed by the Palestine Liberation Front: occupied by Israel

** Claimed by Morocco and Polisario Front: occupied by Morocco

PLUTO   NEPTUNE   SUN   EARTH   MARS

URANUS   JUPITER   VENUS   MERCURY   SATURN

▽ *The world is divided into 24 main time zones. People change their watches by one hour as they cross* *from one zone into another. Time zones are measured east and west of 0° longitude. There is a difference of 24 hours at the International Date* *Line. People crossing this line heading west lose a day. People going east gain a day.*

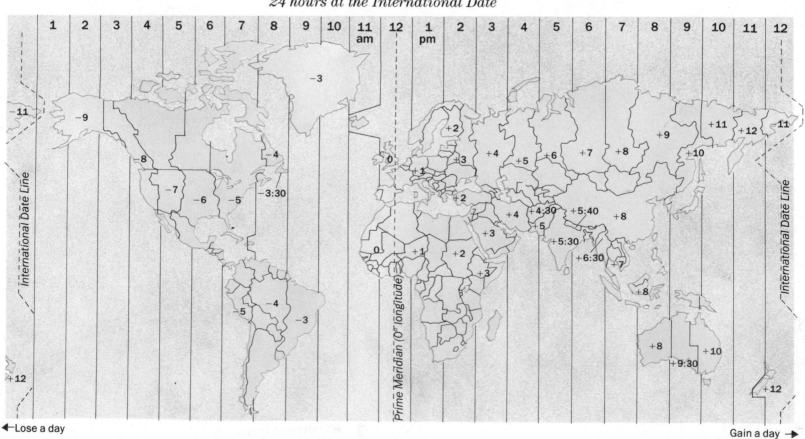

←Lose a day

Gain a day →